Downstairs the room was a p[...]
London bods and provincial girls at their most radiant, aided
slightly by UV lights and hazy vision. Blonde girls with glossy
LA hair, impeccable tans and deep, rounded cleavages encased
within satin skins and feathers; dark girls with sleek-styled bobs
and Audrey Hepburn gamine cuts. The layers of music built up
around them, like a sticky web that enmeshed its captive
listeners, all entranced by a symphony of drugs, heat and the
company of like-minded souls.

Also in the BACKSTREETS series

SLACKNESS
Jonathan Brook

BIG UP!
Jonathan Brook

JUNGLIST
Two Fingers & James Kirk

HERBSMAN
Jonathan Brook

BASS INSTINCT
Two Fingers

THANKS
Iestyn and Josh Wheeler for musical expertise;
Kirsten for posing beautifully and all at Kennington;
Mum, Dad and Finola & Patrick; Marie, Vanessa and
Anne Marie for the moral support; Jake for his patience.
And finally – London – for being the original
home of Nutters

BACKSTREETS

RAISE YOUR HANDS

GERALDINE GERAGHTY

B▨XTREE

First published in the UK in 1996 by
Boxtree Limited
Broadwall House
21 Broadwall
London SE1 9PL

10 9 8 7 6 5 4 3 2 1

Cover Star – Kirsten Wilson
Cover Photo – Eddie Otchere
Cover Design – Martin Lovelock
Series Editor – Jake Lingwood

Typeset by SX Composing, Rayleigh, Essex
Printed and bound in Great Britain by
Cox & Wyman Ltd, Reading, Berkshire

ISBN 0 7522 0166 2

A CIP catalogue record for this book is available
from the British Library

One

A large dark moth head-butted the bare yellow-ing light bulb in the centre of the room, causing an almost indiscernible tremor. A brief wash of light swooped over the circle of still and upturned faces. BB began:

'THE STRAITS ARE DIRE
I'M IN THE MIRE
THROW MY FUTURE ON THE FIRE
REACHING FOR OBLIVION
RIDING ON LIFE'S PILLION
I'M ONE OF THREE MILLION –

and, er, I've got to think of another word rhyming with -illion . . . Anyway – .' He cleared his throat and continued:

'TAKE MY SOUL FOR A DANGEROUS RIDE
DIVE DOWN DEEP INSIDE
CAN'T YOU FEEL MY ANXIOUSNESS
TAKE AWAY MY CONSCIOUSNESS –

and. . .that's as far as I've got.'

'Fucking top' said Wiz.

'Really dark – I like that,' said Virgil.

'Yeah,' said H.

'I thought we could have the vocals really low, so they only register, like, subconsciously.' BB was secretly delighted at the response.

'Yeah . . . I'll pull the fader right down and maybe EQ the top end of it a bit and get a nice little touch of transparent reverb,' said Virgil, his hyper-techno mind already making big plans for their track. He needed to oil the cogs of his mind and went to the dusty tape deck. He switched on and from the speakers came the unearthly sounds of 'Amazon' by World 2 World. This track was a divine revelation in music, truly inspirational. If he could ever come up with something even close to this . . . .

The meeting had started in the seedy back room of the Blue Dog Record shop. The six key, and only, members of the AHL were assembled, as they had been every Thursday night for the past month. Aside from their fledgling musical projects, a common hatred had brought them together, a hatred of the things that, in their eyes, made the world flawed.

'Right,' began BB, their self-appointed spokesman, in his slow hiss of a voice. 'I just want to say, we've had a really good response around town this last week. I got a couple of calls from possible future members, although I will stress that giving out my home number in future is off limits. My mobile is, of course, eligible for calls any time of the day or night if needs be.' He paused, savouring the silence in the small, damp room, then took a hard pull on his eight-skin joint and passed it to the boy on his right, always mindful of impeccable drug etiquette.

'Cheers, Guv,' said the recipient, a small, prematurely balding boy of twenty, known to his friends as Wiz.

BB continued: 'I'm also hoping that my recent Manchester trip may prompt a few new enthusiasts to join in with our little "jollifications".' He paused for the titters he expected whenever he cracked a 'joke'. They didn't come. 'As,' he went on, 'an increase in numbers is just what we need at the moment.'

BB's *t*s were getting more pronounced and Barry and Colin, the inseparable duo to his left, shifted uncomfortably, knowing something was coming their way.

'Which brings me to a little something I think we all know needs a few words said about it –'

'Don't you mean, "About which a few words need to be said"?' piped up Wiz.

BB looked down at him with a withering look, a dirty

'doss' of old, perfected in the third form, when BB first felt threatened by authority figures. 'As I was saying, the attempted abduction of two offenders last week in Gray's Inn Road was not entirely successful. NO –' BB's voice took on it's "John Major in mood" inflection. 'OH, NO . . .WHATT WE ARE TALKING ABOUT HERE IS A COMPLETE FUCKING DISASTER.'

His voice rang around the room. H yawned. The volume of BB's voice softened now, but the rage was still there (at least, in BB's mind).

'There is no pointt in me making a detailed plan of attack if the operants are going to GETT STONED AND FORGETT WHATT FUCKING TIME THEY WERE SUPPOSED TO BE THERE . . . IS THERE? . . . I SAID, IS THERE?'

He glared at the guilty pair, who in turn glared at their fingernails and then at the floor.

It was a long Tennent's swilling, dope-dabbling night, the assembled members churning over their pet hates, each one exorcizing the demons which played on their minds, which disturbed the balance of their individual worlds. They had a vision, free from the spread of the evils they were trying to extinguish – albeit while sitting in their bedrooms in their mums' and dads' houses, getting gip off the old man for being a "lazy, good-for-nothing waster who lived off other people, whose mates didn't have a brain cell between them and never did a bleeding day's work in their lives"'.

Well, the old man was wrong. Now they *were* doing

something, something that would change their lives for the better. They weren't going to put up with people who made them sick any more. The Anti-Handbag League was something they could risk their lives, nay, their very souls for.

Their world was dark and scary and strange, and the skies were full of aliens . . . and these boys liked it that way.

Two

Marly looked out from the steamy window of the lorry on to the pink river as it thundered over Battersea Bridge, heading north. The early light played on the red and golden bricks of the buildings lining the northern bank of the Thames. Benny's B&H blistered and crackled as he sucked hard on the butt. The cumulus of chemical smoke made Marly feel thirsty and ill, so she took one from the box on the dashboard and lit up. At least, she tried to reason, she'd be blowing out more smoke than she was breathing in.

'Do you want a cup of tea, pet?' asked Benny,

lorry-driving rough diamond and friend of her older brother.

'No, I'm all right . . . I'm starving, though. Shall we stop for some breakfast?'

'We'll be all right once I've dropped this lot off. Tony'll sort us out with a fry-up. Fag up for us, will you?'

Marly lit a cigarette from hers and passed it to Benny. His chapped red hand, with its Claddagh ring glinting in the cracked dawn sun, reached out and knocked it from her fingers and in between his legs.

'Get it, will you? For fuck's sack! OWWWW!' he screamed.

Marly laughed and screamed as the lorry swerved all over the road and she groped around Benny's thighs.

'It's not funny . . . Fuck!'

Benny, bright red in the face, shifted and retrieved the bent cigarette and put it in his mouth.

'Jesus,' he sighed.

Marly sat back in her seat. 'Well, that's our excitement for the day, then.'

'It's excitement you're looking for, is it?' He swung the steering wheel over to the right and the lorry lunged towards an oncoming bus.

'Stop it! Stop, for God's sake, Benny.'

Benny pulled up the wheel just in time, as a stream of abuse drifted back to them through the open window of the No. 19.

'You're weird,' said Marly.

'In fact all Bennys are weird . . . It's the *Crossroads* curse.'

The lights turned red as they came up to the King's Road. Out of the window Marly saw a thin, poised woman fussing over two identical designer dogs in the leafy patch of garden outside her house. The woman looked up in distaste as the lorry squealed and belched out exhaust and the animals wriggled and cowered.

'God, she looks like a bitch,' said Marly.

'Love to see inside that house, though.'

The woman's head turned at the sound of a thumping car stereo coming up towards the lights. A white Ford Escort screeched up next to the lorry and the two dogs started barking insanely. The woman dragged them in, giving the car a stony stare and slamming the Georgian door behind her. Marly looked down at the car, crammed full of girls and boys, looking white-faced and washed-out. The 4-4 beat din ticked and thumped, filtering through the two cars.

Benny's fingers drummed in time on the leather seat. Marly strained to hear the muffled sample,

'H*ear the music* . . . H*ear the music*',

and watched them all nodding identically, not speaking to one another and gazing at nothing in particular. A pallid blond boy pulled on a joint, while the girl next to him was trying to roll another. The boy suddenly looked up at the lorry and caught Marly's eye. She smiled and he started winding down his window as if to pass her the joint. The light changed as he tried to clamber out and reach the lorry, and the girl next to him grabbed his arm and pulled him back in as the Escort revved up and sped off ahead.

Marly had a sudden homesick pang, thinking of her mates back home, who would spend nights out like that, aimlessly driving around looking for a micro-morsel of hash or grass, if for nothing else, to enliven nights at the local in her small, shaggy little town. Now she was in London, all that seemed a little sad and distant.

Secretly she hoped to begin her real life here, the one she'd been planning and dreaming of since she was fifteen. Trips to London had been scarce in the past, always merely passing through on the way to big, rowdy family weddings in Ipswich or Kent. Her only English friend had lived in the country, which to Marly seemed identical to home, with its slow pace and incessant gossipmongering.

All these years she had nurtured a private dream that London's landscape offered innumerable paths of opportunity. Surely she had only to choose the right one to find happiness.

Benny's drop-off was a fitted kitchen to be delivered to a house in Victoria. He would have to go back and fit the fucker, he said, but not until he'd stopped at Tony's in Kilburn for a bath and some food.

'Tony has a phone, hasn't he?'

'Get to fuck, of course he does. What did you think, a couple of yoghurt pots on a string? God, he has a mobile *and* a pager now.'

'Oh . . . What does he do?' asked Marly.

'On the rock and roll.'

They were now passing some grand monument, turning left into Park Lane. Marly stared at the giant figures looming blackly against the morning sky on top of the arch.

'God, that's beautiful,' she breathed. 'That's what I'd like to have in my garden . . . Imagine waking up to it every morning.'

'You'd have a fucking stiff neck, that's for sure,' replied Benny, killing the moment.

Park Lane was already jammed with traffic. To her left, Marly watched the joggers jolting and shaking their ageing bones through the park. She laughed as she imagined the response at home if any of the old ones suddenly adopted fitness regimes and began racing through the village every morning. The walk down to the pub was exertion enough.

Rounding Marble Arch they turned up the Edgware Road and Benny pulled in for more cigarettes and a paper.

'Would you nip out and get them? They'll stick me with a ticket if I stop at the lights over here.'

Marly jumped down from the cab and ran into an Iranian supermarket, catching a few tongue-clicks and wolf-whistles from the twenty-four hour café next door. She knew she wasn't looking particularly attractive after a night on the ferry and turned and glared at the men, who took this as encouragement.

'Hey, lady. Hey, you wan' sit wi' uz?'

Back in the lorry, she shut her eyes and pulled her jacket around her shoulders.

'Wake me up when we're there.'

Tony lived above a bookie's on Kilburn High Road. It was in between an Indian and an off-licence, so he was nicely set up, Benny told her almost enviously.

'Marl, wake up. We're here.'

Marly's face dropped as she took in the ragsy dump of Kilburn, lined with dirt, like the face of one of its own tramps.

'God, I hope Chalk Farm is better than this,' she prayed.

'ALL RIGHT, YOU WANKER!' came a resonant bellow from the steps.

Tony was as sublimely charming as ever, Marly noted. Not wanting to criticize her countrymen, she had to admit that the Irish weren't really *that* funny, certainly not as funny as everyone made out.

After breakfast, during which Tony kept pretending to cry and taking both their hands saying, 'This is just *so* beautiful . . .' and 'You guys . . .' while bursting into mock tears and giggles, Benny went off for a soak.

Tony rolled endless joints and Marly got more stoned than she wanted. Eventually, after Benny's departure to Victoria and Tony bringing out his bong, she made her moves to leave.

'I must phone Kate,' she said after a long sigh.

Kate had left for work, but her chirpy flatmate, Lee welcomed her in her loud Colchester husk telling her to come round, she'd be in, she'd look after her, sort her out, make her at home . . . .

'OK. See you in a bit, then,' said Marly, putting down the phone, suddenly exhausted. She was looking forward to this flat with Kate, a friend from her year in France. They'd kept in touch the way most people want to but never do. Now, with a room free and Marly climbing the walls at home after college, they'd arrived at the perfect arrangement. Marly had saved all summer from her waitressing job to get the first month's rent and a bit on the side until she found something in London. Kate was from a genteel Somerset family, quite well to do, as far as Marly could make out, a little dappy, but generous and kind. They'd met as au pairs, living in the same apartment block in Bordeaux. One morning Kate had knocked on her door, asking for a cigarette, and they'd chatted for hours.

'Oh, thanks, darling. I knew you were English, well amost. You just had a certain "I dunno wot", as we say in Yeovil.'

Marly had thought she looked like a pale, spindly angel standing there in the morning sunlight, all white limbs and candy-floss hair. Together they'd fallen in love with locals, had their hearts broken and lived through it to slag off Frenchmen. Over the last few years they'd made regular visits to one another in Dublin, where Marly was studying, or Somerset. The latter were invariably 'out of yer 'ead' weekend binges in a field near Stonehenge with Kate's country mates, whose mothers looked astonishingly young, dressed like Stones groupies and smoked dope with their kids – something which still surprised Marly, even though she knew it was uncool to show it. All the same, the thought of *her* mum skinning up, going glassy-eyed and complaining about the size of her deal gave her the creeps.

Marly said goodbye to Tony, promising to ring him and introduce him to her new flatmates, because in his own words, he was 'desperate for a shag and not ashamed to admit it'.

She walked down Kilburn High Road, marvelling at the endless string of shops selling piles of imitation marigolds and bin-liners, and, following Tony's instructions, caught the No. 31 bus to Chalk Farm. She'd been well primed on the Irish hang-outs in London, but Kilburn seemed like Paddy Hell – the place where all the misfits and malcontents ended up.

She struggled with her bags on to the crowded bus. No one offered a hand even when the handle of one split and she thought how that would never happen at home – her first lesson in London life. She missed her stop and dragged herself back along Camden High Street, past the Lock and down Chalk Farm Road, finally arriving feeling exhausted and a little hard done by.

Kate's flat was above a second-hand clothes shop, full of Hawaiian Elvis shirts and fifties evening dresses, along with the habitual leather- and suede-jacket rack being ransacked by a bunch of Indie-kid students.

She rang the side bell and a bunch of keys came careering down from the first-floor window. Marly let herself in, dragging her bags and knocking over a mountain bike propped up against the wall. A boy popped his head round the door of the ground-floor flat, bring with him a blast of The Mad Professor's sultry dub with the bass turned up to a Spinal Tap eleven. The stranger had a pale, pasty complexion, with thick, matted dreadlocks, but his eyes were bright green and friendly.

'Yeah. . . um, sorry, yeah. I meant to bring it in last night, but you know . . . huh, uhh huhg.'

Marly smiled. 'I'm looking for Kate and Lee's.'

'Oh, right . . . Yeah, first floor and it's the . . . umm . . . right-hand door. D'you need a hand with your stuff?'

The front door was wide open and the wails and shrieks from a tune she'd heard before came sailing through from the kitchen, with Lee's hoarse accompaniment on the chorus,

'My . . . *heart . . . heart beats like a dr* –

Oh, hi. Come in, then. I'm Lee, Very nice to meet you and all that.'

She reached over, turned the tape down and took a drag on her Marlboro Light, smoothing the tendrils of her feather cut at the sides of her head. She looked at Marly with wide, limpid hazel eyes. Her face was not beautiful in the conventional sense, but captivating in its sparkle and shine.

'Bit out of date, this,' she apologized over the track. 'But I've got a real soft spot, reminds me of my holiday. Well, sit down, then. There's some tea in the pot. D'you want a cup, Rover?'

'No thanks. I'm waiting on someone. I'll see you later.' The boy from downstairs shuffled out of the door, tripping over some silver platform sandals as he went.

'Ooops, sorry,' he mumbled, embarrassed, shutting the door behind him.

Lee slumped down on a chair opposite Marly, stubbed out her cigarette and flashed a quick nervous smile.

'He's a bit of a wanker, isn't he? He's all right, though. Gets me really cheap grass from these mates of his in Stockwell. I think they all take the piss out of him 'cause they're black and he wants to be.'

'Why's he called Rover?'

'Well, according to Paul – he's the guy that lives with us – when Rover was a kid he barked like a dog before he could talk. Something to do with his mum leaving him on his own with the family pet a bit too often.'

Marly laughed and Lee watched her with shrewd eyes, as if already trying to assess her.

'So, how d'you get that name, then? What is it, out of *Christmas Carol* or something? Some ghost, isn't it?'

'No, worse. My mum had a thing about Marlene

Dietrich. I think she saw *The Blue Angel* when she was expecting me.'

'That's nice, that is. Marlene. Yeah, I like it. My mate's a transvestite, you know, drag and all that. He does these terrible impressions of Marlene Dietrich singing that one, you know, "Vat am I to do, I can't elp it", and he does Cilla Black and fucking Marti Caine.' She laughed her raucous laugh.

Lee's Colchester youth had stood her in good stead for life on the London club circuit. From the age of fourteen she'd been flitting around the Essex clubs, picking up tips on the art of blagging, learning lessons about how to win friends and influence bouncers. Those early teenage weekends had been spent showing of her new pubescent curves with her mates, pulling older blokes at all the local hotspots – Cinderellas, Woodsides, Rios. The objects of desire then had been the blokes with the coke, cars and Armani shirts, while her boy peers were still in Lee jeans and Tacchini tops, playing football and hanging around the bus depot. The excitement then lay in the conquest of the slickest Mediterranean-looking bloke around, the one who'd taken her down to London at the weekend, to Stringfellows, the Wag, Xenons, or to his mates' flats for coky jacuzzis, where she'd become the confidante of bigger London girls who worked in PR or music management and looked upon her as something of a novelty. All this was a big thrill for such an eager and curious Lolita.

She still played some of those old jazz-funk and

soul tunes – 'Juicy Fruit', 'I Found Loving' and the embarrassing 'Ooops Upside Your Head' – whenever she wanted to remember her early days, the days of pastel stils, box-pleat skirts and V-back jumpers.

When house took over in her local clubs, she found she took more of an interest in what was actually being played by that once inconspicuous bloke in the corner.

At seventeen she found herself in London in pursuit of one of those swarthy sophisticates she'd met on a night out, but she quickly realized he was small fry. By then she'd found her feet anyway, making friends easily in every club she went to. She was the original E baby. Her formative years had shaped her for its endless capacity for enjoyment. She left behind her peers, who'd joined the ranks of outdoor ravedom, content to 'have it' all night in some draughty aircraft hangar. Instead Lee dived straight into the so-called chic of grown-up London nightclubs. She preferred to pop her pills in comfort. More than anything else, she loved to be happy, and finding a magic bullet to enhance her already bright spark was a class-A result.

Three

'Come on. I'll show you your hovel.'

They dumped the bags and Lee helped Marly unpack. She needed to buy a lamp and a mirror, so Lee took her up the road to Camden. She got what she needed from a po-faced Goth in the Stables market and then went for a drink in the Good Mixer. The pub was half full of old men watching sport on the TV, sinking pint after pint on their meagre Giros. A few young peacocks, dressed to kill in tailored Mod suits, sat in the other bar and eyed the two girls with vague interest, then went back to themselves. Lee bought a couple of pints and they took them outside to sit in the warm late August sun. Marly skinned up some of the grass Tony had given her and a nearby drunk watched with old and rheumy eyes.

'I'll tell your mammies if you don't give us a pull on that,' he wheezed as he stumbled past.

They strolled down to the canal to smoke the joint and sat by the water's edge near a group of stoned French crusties.

'Eh . . . .girlz, has you got some more shit?' one of them called out.

'If you are referring to my narcotics, then I suggest you buy your own, you ponce,' shouted Lee in a posh accent. 'Bloody tourists,' she grumbled to Marly. Then, 'Oh, God, I didn't mean you . . .'

Marly just laughed.

They sunbathed for a while, Lee hitching up her skirt, to the delight of the French boys, then walked home slowly, dizzy from the sun and the smoke. Paul was due in at three and he didn't have keys. As they strolled, Marly talked about her plans for a job in a small production company which was co-run by a guy she'd met back in Dublin.

'That's great,' said Lee. 'If it doesn't work out, though, you could always get a job with me in market research. It's up in Farringdon. The money's all right *and* you can sign on.'

There was no sign of Paul outside, but they heard a loud, abrasive laugh coming out of Rover's as they came into the hall. Lee called out and Paul appeared, leaning against the door-frame, tall and thin and brown, with tired eyes, after a night without sleep.

'How was Club Me?' asked Lee.

'Shit . . . Stella Dave was supposed to play but he didn't turn up. It was all industrial German crap and the chill-out room was boring Goa trance. I just went back to Adam's and did some acid and pissed about on his decks. Give us the keys, then.'

He traipsed up the stairs in front of them and let himself in, going straight to the bathroom for a shower.

Marly felt a little put out at the lack of acknowledgement. Lee read her thoughts.

'He's always like that after a heavy night. You'll really like him once you get to know him. Now . . . what shall we have for dinner?'

Paul's past was as chequered as that of most boys of twenty-four. On the dole for the last two years, he'd supplemented his income with a bit of dealing and a spot of painting and decorating, as well as a few DJing nights at small clubs and parties. Like a million others, he refused to join the workforce because he had a dream of his own and he intended to survive any way he could until it was realized.

His schooldays in Croydon had been squandered in the usual wastrel way; smoking away the study periods, bunking off for weeks on end, then the horrible blazing rows at home when the letter of reprimand finally arrived from school. He left as soon as he could, staying with a girlfriend until he found a job at a

City bank. At first he ran errands, graduating to dealing in bonds and later cocaine to his less streetwise, upper-class-slummer colleagues. The lifestyle carried him up on a wave of empty romances with wannabe glamour models, shaky friendships cemented in the toilets of City wine bars and the endless acquisition of objects of desire. He had thought his life was second to none and gradually lost contact with his south London connections, including his family, until one night in the middle of a particularly heavy binge he picked up the phone, wired to the teeth, and was told of his father's second, and fatal, heart attack. He hadn't seen him in over a year. Paul spent a long time at home, feeling he needed to leave the world behind him, at least for a while.

His salvation was his love of music and it became his mainstay. He used his third of his father's insurance wisely, buying equipment and eventually moving in with his girlfriend, the former occupant of Marly's room. The relationship lasted precisely six months, until she went off with a crystal-sniffing club promoter, breaking his concentration for a while but not his heart.

Lee and Kate had asked him to stay. They'd never liked Francesca anyway, they said. Besides, they needed him to protect them from Rover and 'each other'. He agreed, secretly loving the fuss they made of him, which was like having two mums without the nagging. His next step was to find proper premises to set up a studio with his mates from home.

Now he came into the living room and threw his fags down on the table with his customary sigh, falling back on the couch next to Marly. He looked about the room as if something wasn't quite right, then sparked up and offered her one. She smiled nervously and took it, but he didn't look up. She was waiting for a sign. He got up and turned on the TV. This was one of the things she would get used to: that you could walk into a house and there were no niceties of any kind, no deliberate hospitality. You knew you would get talking sooner or later, but it didn't really matter.

They watched in silence until suddenly Paul started shouting at the TV, as if it was the most natural thing on earth, but also as if she was already part of the furniture, which she supposed was his way of making her feel at home.

They watched a daytime women's-magazine show with an overweight 'caring' presenter who stared at the camera with an expression Paul said he'd like to wipe off, looking slightly unhinged, and announced this week's edition was 'Fat women can be beautiful too'.

Paul started to wreak his verbal wrath on Americans: 'People listen more to shows like this in America than they do to their own consciousness, don't you think?' He carried on before she had a chance to answer, 'They've stopped thinking for themselves over there. England's becoming exactly the same. They watch shows like this to solve their fucking problems. About half the country doesn't vote . . . Can you believe that?

And the other half treats elections like they're some kind of Oscar ceremony. Now we've got England giving votes to the fucking homeless, saying they can finally help themselves. What a fucking joke. England's turning, I'm telling you, We thought the eighties were bad. It's going to get worse before it gets better.'

'And what are you going to do about it?' said Marly.

He laughed. 'I don't know yet . . . do you want a cup of tea?'

Kate was back at seven. After a few minutes of screaming and hugging, they sat in the kitchen watching Lee make dinner and smoked and talked, while Paul provided a little cocktail-hour music on his decks.

His random set swung from Biz Mark E to the Fun Boy Three up to Elvis, at which Lee screamed that she just couldn't listen to music her old man was into. Paul, however, was no music snob. He loved anything with a sense of hypnosis – a catchiness that got you by the bollocks, as he delicately put it.

Marly noticed the way that everyone would go silent when certain records came on. It was a feeling of *having* to listen to it, that you were missing out if you lost one second.

They ate in the living room, sitting on the floor around the table. After which Paul brought out a gram of coke, prompting a scream of delight from Lee. Marly had no time to hesitate as Paul passed her the record sleeve and a rolled-up tenner. The first, and last, time she'd tried it was over a year ago, on her twenty-first, and she had been too drunk to feel anything. Now she waited for something to happen. After five minutes her head began to tighten, her tongue tingled and a numbness spread around her face. She started gabbling about her horoscope in the paper that morning. The others had long since learned to control the urge to talk rubbish and Marly felt a little embarrassed.

'Come on. Let's go to the pub. I'm dying for a vodka,' said Lee.

They played pool in the local, joining up with a crowd of Kiwis for a game of Killer, which Paul won, and he bought the next two rounds. Lee flirted outrageously with the only Maori among the posse of New Zealanders.

'He's gorgeous. Prettier than me,' she told Marly in the loos. 'D'you reckon I should ask him back or shall we go out with them? His mates were talking about some club in Oxford Street. One of them touristy ones – Jackie's or Sammie's. I told them not to bother. My friend Philippe and his lot are going down the Undergrowd tonight. What d'you reckon? Am I being a right slag? What do you want to do?'

Marly laughed. 'I don't mind. I'm up for anything.'

'Yeah, well, we'll have to get some more drugs. That Charlie's worn off and the Underground's on till four.'

Four

From the street, it looked like any other surburban house, but a short walk down the alley at the side and suddenly it was visible: a small lock-up garage with sludge-green doors, the paint peeling through neglect, covered in schoolboy graffiti. A step nearer and you could hear the hushed murmurs coming from within. An urban fox rummaged around a bin nearby and tipped it over, making a tinny clash.

'What was that? Wiz, check it out,' ordered BB, sitting inside on an old fusty armchair pilfered from a skip. Wiz crept over to the spyhole and stood on a plastic crate to peer into the Pinner night. Numbers had not increased as BB had hoped in the past week or so, very possibly due to the idea of free drugs in return for devotion to the group being abandoned. BB dismissed this as unimportant; the real strength lay in the founder members, the true believers. The hard-core Anti-Handbag League had faith in their top boy, even if they hadn't yet actually managed to pull off any of their plots to destroy the world they so despised, the world of happy house.

'I don't like this,' whispered Col, red-eyed and pasty-faced, his pot paranoia getting the better of him. 'My dad's gonna kill me if he finds us here.'

Wiz turned around, still teetering on the crate.

'It's cool, snuffink there,' he assured them in his speedy whine.

'Right. Now, you all know,' began BB, 'why you're here, so I just want to go through some last-minute details. Baz and Col, you're sorted for the van to be outside the venue at three-thirty. Myself, Wiz and Virgil will be at the warehouse, making preparations, while H,' he said, referring to the silent, smiling, secretly tripping boy in the corner, 'will be in the venue, with his *girlfriend* –' He spat the word out – 'and keeping an eye on any likely candidates.'

H broke out of his rose-tinted reverie to acknowledge his role in the proceedings. 'Yeah . . . No problem. Keep 'em peeled and all that. Huh, huh, huh.'

'Now, you've got the supplies I bought and you're happy with the layout of the place. So, any extra punishments you might like to inflict are very much welcome. All that's left to be said is good luck and see you around four. Wiz, Virg, let's get moving.'

BB set off with his beat boys and closed the door behind him. The room suddenly warmed up without his presence.

'Oi, skin up, Baz,' said Col.

H put a cassette in the battered Matsui tape player and a remix of Black Fog's 'Coughing Nails' filled the room with its bleak underground techno curl.

'Nice track,' said Baz, licking his lips to wet his Rizla and nodding away to the murky beat amid its background of road drills and snapping springs.

'Yeah, it's right cheeky, this one,' replied H, the music binding with all the thoughts racing around his acid-riddled brain.

They settled back to wait for their time and drifted off into the opiate sounds that made their lives worth living.

The ritual of dressing up was far more elaborate than Marly was used to. Lee washed her hair for the second time that day. It had to be wet to style it just right, she insisted. Kate put on some music in her bedroom while they dressed, a prelude to the club, while Paul and Lee's New Zealander sat in the kitchen comparing the quality of drugs in their respective cities.

'I need a pair of tights . . . Who's got a pair of tights? All mine are ripped. Look, every single bloody pair,' panicked Lee.

'Lee, have you still got my Morgan top, the one I lent you on Tuesday, with the flowers on it? You know, the *really expensive* one?'

'Oh, shit. Sorry, yeah . . . I meant to wash it. Honest.'

'What are you going to wear, Marly?'

'Dunno . . . I've got this, but –' She held out a short, floral summery dress. Lee looked at the garment with a fashion doyenne's wince.

'Here, try this. It's really sexy.'

She handed her a pale yellow Lycra dress, tight, figure-forming.

'It's a Hervé Léger design,' said Lee knowingly.

'You mean rip-off,' said Kate.

'W*here* are my eyelash-curlers?'

'What d'you think of this lipstick? It's too red and slutty, isn't it?'

'No, red's in. Anyway, you can get away with it with your skin.'

'I *need a* HUH HUH HUH HIDEAWAYYY'

The vocals came sailing through the house from Kate's stereo. The three girls were in a good mood as they primped and masked up, performing their little offices unintentionally in time to the music.

By the end of the song, Marly had finished her make-up and went into the lounge, keen to get an appraisal from Paul and, more importantly, to have a pre-departure cigarette to calm the nerves she always got before a big night out.

Paul glanced at her and cracked a smile as she came in but said nothing, while Stuey the Maori stared unashamedly. Lee came bounding in and his object changed.

'Right,' she said breezily. 'Shall we get cabs?'

'Ah, no way. The tubes are still running. It's only six stops,' said Paul. 'I'm skint.'

'Well, I'm getting a cab, and so's Kate and Marly, and you, Stu, so we'll get a black one. Make's no difference. Come on, you tight arse.'

They walked up the road and hailed one round the back of Camden Lock. The cab had a No Smoking sign, so Lee hung out of the window with her fag most of the way.

'I hate these bloody bullyboys who don't let you smoke or bring bottles in their cabs. The amount you pay –'

'I heard that,' said the cockney cab driver, who for once looked and sounded like Dick Van Dyke.

'Yeah? Good. I've just about –' began Lee.

Kate whacked her. 'Don't start, Lee. Um, Tottenham Court Road, please.'

'God, you're such an arse-licker, Kate,' said Lee in mock defiance.

'Yeah, and you're such a fucking rebel, Lee,' replied Paul, ruffling her immaculate hair, which sent her into a frenzied rage.

The journey took in the usual London sights. First there was a fight outside the Camden Palace between a couple of apy bouncers and some sixteen-year-old cheeky-monkey ravers. Next a quick celebrity spot at the lights in Euston Road of two Aussie soap stars in the next cab, who Paul and Stuey wanted to get out and abuse. Then finally up Gower Street and New Oxford Street to Charing Cross Road, with its hordes of tourists wandering slowly and aimlessly around after taking in a show or an Angus Steak, killing time before they went back to their duplicate hotels. For some reason, Marly always connected those steak-houses with Brummies. She'd once met a couple from Dudley in Dublin who had raved about the value for money and asked if they had them in Ireland: 'They're vary raysonible . . . You can git a luvlay prawn cock-tayle, a graaate staayke and any choice of dissert you loike, all for foive nointy-foive. Proper food, thad is.'

They got out at the Dominion, which was showing *Godfather – the Musical*, and walked round the corner to the club. A large queue milled and swayed outside.

Philippe, Lee's Brazilian friend from work, was near the front. 'Oh, Babeee. How are you? Why you not in today? I miss you at lunch.' He kissed her three times and linked arms, waiting to be introduced.

Paul looked a little sheepish shaking hands with the big, brash queen. Marly smiled, dying to laugh at the world of difference between the lad and the mincer. She and Kate received kisses next.

'Oh, honey, I love your dress. Looks soo goood. I've gotta couple like that for my drag show, but with a little more . . . "carrrumba", if you know whad I mean. But, you know, my ass looks so saggy now.' He patted his rear, tightly encased in a pair of red rubber jeans. 'I just gotta start riding my mountain bike again, but I'm so lazy, you know. I don't even go to my step class any more.' He touched his chest and looked at one of the bouncers coyly. 'Are we gonna stand here all night? Come on. My friend Stevie's inside already. I can get two of you in free, so you can split it, OK?'

They sidled past the bouncers, who were choosing their prey for the night, to pull or persecute. Their power was absolute, girls were preparing to sell their souls for ten minutes in return for a freebie or the guest list the following week.

On the way to the cloakroom, Lee slipped Marly an E. 'I'm just going to do half now and see if it's worth staying,' she mumbled, biting hers in two.

'Oh, right . . . um –' There was a flicker of indecision. 'Is Kate having one too? Marly figured there was safety in numbers.

'Yeah, course. What? You don't want it?' said Lee in a babyish voice.

'No, no . . . I do. Do you want some money?'

'No, don't be stupid. It's your first night here . . . any-way Philippe's buying.'

Downstairs the room was a pool of shimmering flamingos. London bods and provincial girls at their most radiant, aided slightly by UV lights and hazy vision. Blonde girls with glossy LA hair, impeccable tans and deep, rounded cleavages encased within satin skins and feathers; dark girls with sleek-styled bobs and Audrey Hepburn gamine cuts. The layers of music built up around them, like a sticky web that enmeshed its captive listeners, all entranced by a symphony of drugs, heat and the company of like-minded souls.

A tinkle touch of piano in minor key triggered off waves of pleasure among the dance floor's throng. Marly felt it would be hard to restrain yourself, for the sake of cool, even if you wanted to. The feeling of 'I love this, you, everyone, the night.' A remake of 'Weekend' came on with its disco strings and caused a frenetic rush from those who'd been sitting it out. Everyone wanted a bit of this one:

'GONNA FIND A FRIEND . . . TO SPEND THE WEEK-END –'

Kate went to the bar to get them drinks. Paul saw some friends hanging around the DJ box and went to say hello. Marly watched the dancers and was slowly drawn in. They drank their beers, waiting for the inevitable tingle to start playing on their bodies as the drugs took effect. The girl on her right was complaining about the lack of talent in the room. Her friend replied it was still early. The boy behind Marly grabbed her round the waist and whispered, 'You look *fab*.'

'Yeah, mate,' said Lee. 'Give us a chance for this pill to kick in and we might think the same about you.'

The set changed. Barry Dumpling was on the decks now, to the crowd's delight. His name buzzed around the dance floor as he put on track after track of happy holiday tunes. Marly and the girls gave themselves up to that indescribable feeling that was different each time, but never as good as the first time. She knew her limits and this was a moment for abandon.

They danced along with shoving boys and girls, all trying to be the best, to shine the brightest, to have a better time than the last. Two blokes were trying to hit on their group in a devious, luvdup way. Paul spotted this from the bar and laughed, but his eyes were detached and liquid and he couldn't concentrate on them for long.

'TONIGHT IT'S PARTY TIME. IT'S PARTY TIME TONIGHT –'

Marly's head was full now, full of the drug, full of abstract thoughts about home, about how she must get some new clothes, about her old boyfriend, and about how the girl next to her kept digging her in the ribs with her PVC handbag as she danced. For some reason Russ Abbott's 'What an atmosphere' kept pounding around her head. She went off to the loos to have a breather.

The three small cubicles were packed, two apiece, with girls powdering up, having a chat, topping up their nightly quotas. The queue was fifteen strong, everyone gazing at each new addition, checking out each outfit, figure, face, hairdo with practised scrutiny. Marly felt a little dowdy next to these supermodel wannabes.

'God, you're really brown, aren't you?' said one to her new friend.

'Yeah, I've been on the sunbed since I got back from Portugal.'

'I dunno. You know, I'm a bit scared of all that these days.'

'Well, I got this stuff from Guerlain. Hyper-filter bodyguard sun crème.' She pronounced it the French way.

'Apparently Nadja and Christy use it and they're as fair as I am.'

'Oh, right.'

'I use that. Really good, isn't it?' offered a stranger, washing her hands.

'I go to this sun booth thing too. You just stand in it for five minutes a time, really intensive, and they play music and that . . . Oh, I love this.' She switched back into dance floor as 'Everybody Wants to be Somebody' came wailing from the other room.

'Gotta get out there. See you later.'

Marly gave up and used the men's, then made her way back to the others, walking carefully through the crowd, a stiff smile on her face which she could do nothing about. She had forgotten about the pill now and felt like she was swimming through a liquid mass of bodies. She even found herself holding her breath until she reached the other side and got to Lee and Paul, who were leaning on one another, sharing a fag and a bottle of water. Kate had made a new friend and was laughing with him. José was from Martinique, a tall, gorgeous model. He was raving on about Edinburgh and its club scene.

'. . . And I love those small Scottish men. You know, really rough-looking guys who go to Rangers matches, preferably wiz a criminal record and lots of, how you say, taboos.'

Kate bent double with laughter and Marly left them to it and drifted over to Philippe and his friend Stevie, who were dancing at the front near the DJ.

'Honey, how's your E?'

'Lovely, thanks.'

'This is Stevie. He makes a lot of fantastic sheets. You know, for the walls in clubs . . . My Gaaad, I gotta get a drink.'

Stevie was off with the fairies after three pills, but smiled sweetly and squeezed her arm. A girl who seemed to know him, came up, her eyes as big as saucers and grinning like a maniac. She hugged Stevie. The show of affection was sweet, but sweet like saccharine, unnatural in one way, but really just another chemical to add to all the others in the human body, Marly told herself. She had a flicker of worry about stories of long-term effects, but it passed as a rump-shaking anthem whipped the crowd into a frothy peak.

'LOVE ME . . . HOLD ME –'

People sang along, raising their eyes and hands in the air, to grasp the feeling as if it were something more solid and permanent than just one night.

Five

Across town on Clapham High Street stood H. He looked around at the clubbers in the queue for State of Disgrace, a club he had recently joined on the orders of BB. It never ceased to raise a smile when he looked at the state of some of them. Boys wearing dark eyeliner, feathers in their hair, freezing their bollocks off in Michael Hutchence clone skirts or, worse still, those with no arse in their trousers. Skinny, poncy runts the lot of them, thought H, simpering at one another with their Japanese designer girlfriends who hung on to their every word. H heard the communal worship in their voices as they overenthused about Ricky Suntan's set in Ibiza last summer.

'Yeah, I was mashed that night. I didn't even do that many pills.'

'I know what you mean. That was a blinder . . . *Four hours*, he played.'

Cunts, thought H.

Simone, his girlfriend, was complaining now. 'I thought we were gonna go to Medieval Torture tonight, H. The bloke doing this club can't mix or nothing,' she said a little too confidently for his liking.

'How would you know?' he said cruelly. 'I've never taken you anywhere he's being playing.' Rumbled, Simone tried to cover up the fact she'd been frequenting a couple of glam house clubs of late with her mates from work, mainly because H hardly ever wanted to see her and, more importantly, because it was more fun than sitting in one of his miserable mates' houses all night, talking about techno and taking far too many drugs.

'Oh, umm, I read a review of it in H*it the Decks*.'

'Yeah, right,' he sneered, looking up to the front of the queue to see how long he'd have to put up with her gip. He was just beginning to feel the full effect of that trip he'd necked earlier. He suddenly remembered he was skint. 'How much cash you got, babe?' he asked her tenderly.

'I thought *you* were taking me out tonight.'

'Naa, I had to pay my mum off for the phone bill, didn't I. And I shelled out the rest of my cash on this

poncy get-up.' He looked down at the tight white PVC
strides BB had made him wear to blend in as one of
'them', and scratched his chest under the tight black
mohair vest, nicked by Baz for the occasion from Kevin
le Cock's boutique in Covent Garden.

'Well, I've got my cash-point card, but –'

'Give us it, then. You get paid Fridays, don't you?'

She handed it over with a sigh.

As Baz and Col wearily tidied up Col's dad's garage,
picking up spliff butts and the odd can of Super Cider,
BB walked around the bare, bleak interior of the warehouse in Bow they had chosen as a suitable 'chamber
of persecution' for the hostages they intended to bring
back later. He nodded with approval.

'Very nice . . . How did you find this, Wiz?'

'Oh, my mate runs a dodgy video business across
the road. He told me it was going empty.'

'Didn't tell him what it was for, did ya?'

'Naaah, mum's the word. You know me.' He winked,
tapping his nose and sniffing hard.

'Give us a hand with this, Wiz,' said Virgil, standing
in the doorway with his decks, speakers, amp and two
silver flight cases full of vinyl. 'I wanna play you this
new track I got today before the others arrive.

Wiz scooted over with his usual boundless, bogus
energy. 'Oh, yeah, what track's that, then, Virg?'

'It's a white label from this geezer in Moers, outside
Cologne. It's wicked . . . It's got this wind-rushing thing
at the beginning, then some sort of clanging bits of

metal sheeting – you know, like cars being made in a factory. I think it's incredible how we're so, like, influenced by our surroundings. 'cause in that part of Europe, of course, it's all automated society, yeah? And they're becoming one with their machines and the music is a product just like anything else. Know what I mean?'

'Err, yeah . . . Where d'you want this, mate?' Wiz struggled under the weight of a 2K speaker.

Waking from some kind of trance, Marly found herself sitting between two guys on the couch in the chill-out room. Long swathes of diaphanous fabric trailed from the ceiling. A few bodies were stretched out on the floor, gazing up smiling at nothing in particular and slyly passing around joints. The boy next to Marly offered her some water and took that as an introduction. He put his fingers together in a Zen-like pyramid cage and smiled.

'Having a good time?' he asked.

His friend sat on her left, slumped, with his head lolling, looking like it was never going to be all right again.

'Is your friend OK?' She peered round at him.

'Oh, yeah,' replied the spiritual one. 'He's just on a buzz at the moment. Let him enjoy it. He's just a really free-flowing guy, you know, like me, going with the buzz and just being.'

'Just being what?' asked Marly, bemused.

'No, just *being*. My yoga teacher taught me this

meditation technique, OK? He calls it Spiritual Osmosis, everyone's doing it now. It was invented by the Yogi, um, Yogi Bear Shamankah, or something. Anyway he teaches that we are all like grains of rice, you know, small and helpless and brittle when left on our own, but capable of expanding from within and becoming soft and warm when immersed in a little love . . . or water, do you see? Anyway since my teacher's been practising it he feels like a whole new person . . . except he's gone completely off rice.'

He breathed out slowly. She suddenly wanted to escape. This bloke was the kind who would sit there all night talking about feeling good and all the while would be sapping everyone else's energy and only *he* would be left feeling good about himself, while you were left feeling drained and bewildered.

'It's like those people who are going around slagging off all this, trying to bring it down and bring us down. You know, there are guys out there who don't want us to come together in the light. They want to spread their darkness all over the place.'

Marly was beginning to feel a bit sick.

'I just don't understand how people can hurt one another over music,' he continued. ''cause music is life, yeah? It heals and nourishes the soul . . . Why would anyone want to destroy that?'

'cause of people like you, probably, thought Marly.

He carried on, oblivious to whether she was listening. 'I mean, Jesus said –'

'Uh, oh. Time to leave,' she murmured.

Luckily, Kate and Lee came looking for her at that moment.

'Me and Stuey are going back to Philippe's. Kate's staying for a bit.'

'What do you want to do? I told Paul I'm going in about half an hour.'

'Let's have a dance.'

While H was attempting to carry out his first 'terrorist' prank of the night, loading the hand-dryers in the men's lavs with itching powder, he found himself in a sticky situation.

'Give us a line of that, mate. I gotta sort me head out,' came a voice from behind.

A large, beefy bruiser stood there, blocking the doorway, muscles bulging in his white Otto Osmosi chiffon shirt. H edged away as the guy bent over the ledge of the sink, chopped out a line and rolled up a twenty. H slipped out of the door to find Simone.

Meanwhile, Baz and Col sat in their van parked in a side alley round the corner from the club.

'Can I have a bit of your Curly-Wurly?' said Col.

'No . . . Buy your own.'

'Oh, cheers, mate. I'll remember that when I open my Quavers.'

The van was six inches deep in ancient copies of the Sun, Coke cans, skins and sweet wrappers.

Baz peered around slowly. 'Look at the fucking state of this. It's a fucking tip. Can't you clear up after you?

I've got to take this to work on Monday. Not a very good fucking example for a car-valet firm, is it?'

They sat in silence for ten minutes while Col crunched his Quavers. Baz glared at him in annoyance and slotted a tape into the stereo.

'Windwalker . . . Red Planet 5, innit, Baz?' said Col, with his mouth full.

'It's 6 . . . Red Planet 6, actually.'

Baz skinned up, taking his kit from the secret panel in the dashboard.

'Shit, I'm nearly out of dope.'

'You're having a laugh. It's only half-two. We're gonna be here at least another hour before H comes out.'

'Fuck it. Phone up your mate in Vauxhall. See if he can sort us out.'

Col's friend told them to come straight round as he was just about to 'go to kip with his bird'. They drove like the clappers and got there just before three.

'This is it,' said Col, as they pulled up before a big housing estate with a map-plan on a big board.

'D'you know your way around here?' Baz shivered as they got out.

'Course. It's the second lot of flats down there.'

They entered the labyrinth. Ten minutes later they were back at the map, scratching their heads.

'BB'll go mad if we miss the pick-up with H. He might even sling us out of the group, Col.'

'Chance'd be a fine thing,' said Col under his breath. 'Right, here we are –' stabbing the map with his finger.

All the lights were off in Darren's flat and Col banged on the door for a few minutes. Darren finally appeared, bleary-eyed, wearing his girlfriend's satin wrap.

'I though you said straight away. My bird's gonna give me untold strife for this.' He nodded towards the bedroom. 'Anyway, what d'you want?'

'Ummm, just a 'teenth, please, Dal.'

'What? You come all this way and get me out of bed for a fucking sixteenth . . . Dear, oh dear.' He tutted his way to a drawer in the kitchen and measured out a tiny bag of grass. 'Right, there you go. I'll see you later.'

''Ere, Dal, d'you reckon I could have a quick cup of tea. I got the right deserts.'

'You're having a Turkish, mate . . . Oh, go on, then, but you're gonna have to make it yourself. I'm off to bed . . . And don't slam the door on your way out.' He padded off into the bedroom.

It was dangerously late when they finally left the flat, having had to wait for Baz, who made a suspiciously long trip to the loo. Col went in to wash his hands after him.

'Fuck me, Baz, what d'you have for tea tonight?' he asked as they walked to the van. Baz stopped.

'The wheels.'

'Eh?' Col sniggered.

'The wheels on the van – they're fucking gone!'

The two desperadoes stood silent and open-mouthed and stared at the four neat piles of bricks under each corner.

'Could be worse, mate,' said Col at last. "At least we've got some fucking gear.'

For the remainder of the night, H managed successfully to dodge the strapping clubber who'd sampled his 'drugs' earlier on. He found Simone with a couple at a table, talking enthusiastically about music.

'Yeah, I love that one. All them strings and that organ bit. Right uplifting and –' Her voice faltered as H approached.

He reminded himself of his goal for the night. These two seemed as likely a pair of victims as anyone in the club. Both loved up, smiling away, she in a pastel baby-doll, he in leather trousers and a tight acid yellow and mauve tank top. BB would most definitely approve.

'All right, mate?' he said to the boy as cheerfully as he could. 'D'you want a beer?'

Marly, Kate and Paul got back to Chalk Farm around four.

'We didn't see much of you tonight, Paulie,' said Kate, putting on some hot milk and chewing a couple of Vitamin C tablets.

'Want one?' She placed it in Marly's mouth.

'Yeah, I met this bloke I used to go to school with. He's trying to do his own music too. We had a good chat about this and that. Turns out he's thinking of renting a studio and asked if I was up for it. He's got somewhere in mind and he's going to put up the cash if I bring in all my gear.'

'Nice one. That's just what you need, darling. Roll us a spliff, will you?'

They sat in Paul's tiny room on his bed, listening to the Tricky album and some trip hop that Fido had given him. 'One of my own,' Fido had announced proudly. They talked about Marly's job prospects in the production company in Soho.

'I know the bloke quite well. He's pretty sound and everything. In the end, it's up to the woman who runs the place. Nick reckons she's looking for an assistant to do all the menial stuff while she goes sailing around town, having production meetings and fishing for new contracts.'

'Sounds all right. As long as she likes you. That's always the main thing with those kinds of companies. You could always do waitressing, though, if you're stuck.'

'Fuck that. I did it for two years at college. I can't face another job full of rude old gits and mad chefs who wank in the food for a laugh and cry on your shoulder 'cause their wife's just kicked them out.'

Kate laughed.

'Bloody hell, what restaurant was that? I'll have to go.'

They sat up till the first birds started warbling shakily outside. Kate kept them amused by reading from a box of old letters from past besotted boyfriends and admirers. The winner of the Most Corny title, Marly and Paul decided, was from Alberto, an Italian ski-lift attendant she'd briefly dallied with on a skiing holiday.

'"My mather says she is very happy I meet a Catolic girl. When I think of your bland hair and sweat smiele, I feel very emotion and the nigt I spen in your rom I fel like a child with it's mather, especially when you . . ."'

'Stop . . . I don't want to hear any more,' said Paul, laughing. 'That's fucking depressing. Euro-romances . . . doomed from the start.'

'Ahhh.' Kate yawned ungraciously. 'I'm going to have a bath and try and sleep.' She kissed Marly. 'You've got enough covers for your bed, haven't you? Right, Night, then.'

She went to kiss Paul. 'On second thoughts –' She grimaced and shut the door behind her with a giggle.

Marly felt a bit edgy now she was alone with Paul. It was nothing she could put into words, so she blamed it on the normal girl/boy/alone/together scenario. She also had an incredible urge to curl up on the bed with him, but she blamed that on the E.

They talked easily enough, Paul enthusing about his 'soon to be' studio and how he planned to meet the guy in the week for a drink and a chat. He played Marly some of his stuff on DAT and she listened silently, thinking he really was quite talented. He had an ear for all kinds of sounds and instruments and pooled all the right ones effortlessly together, playing keyboards himself. The result was a danceable, airy tune, with no screaming vocals to buoy it up. Usually when she listened to music, she couldn't help but pick out bits she thought could be improved, but with this there was nothing left to do. He'd thought of everything.

They drifted off like that and when Marly woke up later that morning, Paul had brought her duvet in and put it over her, while he had lain down on the mattress in her room so as not to wake her. He looked awkward lying there, curled up and covered only with a tiny blanket, with a worried look on his face as he slept. Her heart gave a little twist at his chivalry and she smiled at the thought of friendship to be had in the times ahead.

Baz and Col chewed over the prospect of going back to the warehouse to explain. They decided a café fry-up and then home for a kip was the best plan of action. 'Yeah . . . Give BB a chance to cool off.'

H stood outside the club, doing his best to interest Kyle and Shireen, his two 'hostages', in hanging around with the promise of a 'really blinding party in east London, loads of pills, top music and that', and casually looking up and down the street for Baz's van, telling the pair his mate was due any second and they could all get a lift there. Their patience lasted almost as long as the E buzz they were on and as long as H was handing out the free fags. H's trip was becoming a pain in the arse now. He'd had enough of the sur-roundings and the company: Simone and Shireen were starting to grizzle about the cold in their skimpy outfits.

'Well, why the fuck did you wear it, you stupid cow?' he snapped.

'Birds, eh?' He smiled, shaking his head blokily at Kyle.

'Look, mate, d'you think this mate of yours is coming or what? I'm fucking dying to get another pill inside me. That third one I took was a fucking dud,' he said, referring to the cat-worming tablet H had pressed into his hand at the bar.

'Well, we could get a cab,' panicked H, thinking of the wrath of BB if he didn't show up with the goods.

Tonight meant everything to BB. They were childhood friends (although he'd always been a weird child, even by H's standards) and he didn't want to let him down in his plan to initiate, by force if necessary, those 'lightweight ponces' to the joys of underground techno. BB had introduced H and the rest of his mates to that strange, possessed world and they had signed up without delay, finding it a natural progression from the death metal that had filled their adolescent years. Now BB saw the need for more effective action in the task of spreading the word and had announced his plan one night after a particularly heavy acid-dropping sesh round Col's. The doors of perception of 'how it really is' had opened, BB reckoned, and finally made him realize that the empire of music would fall unless someone put a stop to what he saw as the brash, wanton and downright 'fucking sissy' world of handbag. These two unknowing victims were so close to being subjected to what remained of the night's torture. BB intended to convert them, to forcefeed them with so much propaganda and techno babble they would be left ashamed and repentant of their past frivolity.

'Yeah, but don't you think it's a bit harsh, Guv? I mean, it's a free country and all that?' Baz had countered in the beginning.

'Well, it worked in the fucking war, didn't it?' had been BB's reply.

Kyle spotted a black cab on the other side of the street. 'Listen, mate. Thanks and all that, but I've had enough. I'm chipping off. Come on, Shireen. See you both down here next week or something, yeah?'

They ran over to the taxi, Shireen's feather boa moulting a trail behind her as she ran. They were gone before H had a chance to protest.

'Ahhh, they were really nice,' sighed Simone, picking a stray feather out of her hair.

Back at the warehouse the boys gave it till eight then started slowly packing up. A caretaker would be coming round the building at nine, Wiz had warned. BB's fury was quietly bubbling over at the futility of the night. He'd barely spoken for the past two hours, since he'd realized something was up, but had sat there listening to Virgil mixing his dark, grim, mood-swinging tracks: 'Circus Bells' with its banging 303s filtering up to a high-pitched scream and 'Spastik' with its insane fast drumming, drowning Wiz's incessant drones about a programme he'd seen the night before on UFOs.

BB lifted the last case of records into Virgil's Datsun

Cherry and breathed a long sigh. It was another fucking day, he noted. It looked like a sunny one too. He'd
sleep until the sun went down and then he'd see. After
all, in the distorted words of Scarlett O' Someone,
'Tonight is another night.'

Six

Lee had been waiting all week to blow her wages on a pair of satin jeans she'd seen in *Vogue*. Black, straight, elegant, hip-diminishing, £160. She made it a rule to invest in something quality every month and resist the cheap temptations of chain-store bargain threads, which she thought an appropriate name for them seeing as they fell apart after three washes. Lee had changed her look three times in the past year, from a long, parted-in-the-middle South of France sex kitten do with perma-tan, to a 1960s messy bob, pale skin and lots of smoky eyeliner, to the blunt, short cut she had now. She was happy with this one. Everybody said it suited her and showed off her long neck and shadowy cheekbones. She wrote down the address of the Giorgio Veruco boutique and made a mental note to fit it into the girls' shopping trip.

Saturday was a nightmarish day for it in town, but Kate pleaded it was her only free time, so they set off in the early afternoon, feeling fragile. Lee managed not to complain once through one of the worst comedowns she'd ever had. Easy enough when you were on a mission. She had to have those beautiful trousers; her heart was set on wearing them that night.

South Molton Street and St Christopher's Place first for a browse, then down to Kensington High Street, where Marly got some strappy red leather heels and a couple of tops. Then they were off to the King's Road. The shop assistants, so called because they are there to assist, alternated between glares and air-hostess smiles depending on the shopper's estimated value or, more importantly, their degree of hipness, which was decreed by those very shops in the first place.

In the Garage, a collective of small shops and stalls, Kate bumped into a couple of girls she knew. Dani, she told them afterwards, was on the front desk at the magazine where Kate worked as a PA, while Sheba, her best friend, was an aspiring actress who had just come back from Edinburgh, where she'd been 'working with a new theatre company who were kind of like Berkoff in the kind of stuff they did'.

'What? Perverted, sick and annoying?' Marly wanted

to say, but she didn't and instead smiled an interested smile.

'Are you going to Prune My Roses tonight?' asked Sheba, as they browsed around a stall full of tiny patent-leather skirts and Jackie O sunglasses.

'Dunno,' said Kate. 'There's that thing on at Temple of Doom in south London that Paul was talking about. One of his mates is DJing and he said he'd try and sort out the guest list.'

'Hmmm, I don't know if I fancy that,' said Sheba, surreptitiously looking at herself in the mirror behind Kate. 'I mean, it's a bit "hard" down there, isn't it, and all those ugly boys? I've always found it a bit *dirty*, if you know what I mean.'

'Yeah, go on,' said Dani. 'Come with us, at least for a drink first. I've gotta meet this promoter bloke we went out with last night – Oliver Hines. You know, he runs those Shove It dos. There's one tonight at Pinacoladarada. They've got loads of excellent DJs and we'll get in for nothing.'

'Isn't he the one who got done for kerb-crawling last year in King's Cross?'

'Oh, that. No . . . that was a total fuck-up. Apparently he was waiting for his mate to come out of the 7-Eleven and thought he saw someone he knew and all that. He told me himself. He was really upset. He reckons the police laid into him 'cause he had a nice car and a bit of cash. God, I mean, *you* know what they're like.'

She raised her eyes and tutted.

They went into the heart of town for a drink in Bar

West a little later, after promising to meet the others that night before the club.

Lee went off to phone Rover about some Es he was supposed to be getting for her. 'I don't want to get home and find out he's fucking forgotten again. I want to get it sorted before tonight, otherwise we'll be left with nothing and have to score some £15 aspirins in the club.'

She moaned when she got back. The bar was full of the usual Soho crowd on a weekend. Italian boy tourists sat open-legged with their hands playing around near their crotch areas. They sat at an outside table, all wearing identical Emporio Armani shades, Gucci loafers and pastel Benetton jumpers and stared as the girls went in to order drinks. They shared one Coke between them and chain-smoked Red Marlboros.

In the corner were a group of out-of-town shoppers who were people-watching and making comments on the various outfits that walked past. 'Look at those weirdos,' said the first, sipping her cappucino with pursed, disapproving lips, as a couple of fairly innocu-ous-looking New Wave punks walked past. Her friends giggled provincially. 'Urgh,' said one.

As Marly paid for the drinks there was a typical Soho couple at the bar who were slagging off a Guns N' Roses video on MTV. The witchy girl, sleek and groomed like a skinny thoroughbred, was delivering a liturgy on the male psyche.

'Look at them,' she sneered as Axl and Slash rock-

postured and pouted their hearts out. 'It's just so typically *male*, the whole dick-power, sexist bullshit. God,
did they realize how *outré* that was even then?'

'Yeah, God, I mean, if that's being a man, then I want
out,' jeered her catty camp companion with a loud
nasal laugh.

Marly felt like telling them to shut the fuck up. They
sat there, tearing to pieces anything that didn't fit into
their small, style-conscious universe. They gave Marly
a good searching appraisal as she stood there. The girl
looked like the type who didn't like other females
around and scorned the men she met in a boring 'all
men are bastards' school of thought.

As the afternoon melted into evening, Lee downed
her Bloody Mary in two gulps and ordered another,
while Marly and Kate sipped at their pints. Marly was
beginning to feel the effects of last night in full.

'I'm getting a few little twinges now,' she com-
plained.

'You've got to carry on. You'll be all right after a
couple more drinks and a smoke. Kerry's bringing
down some Charlie tonight from home.'

Lee's two best mates from Colly, as they all referred
to their home town, were due down later at the flat for
their big night out. The three girls made an effort to try
to meet up at least once a fortnight to go clubbing
together and keep up the hilarity of their little youth-
ful scrapes.

'There's something about when we get together,'

she told Marly and Kate. Me, Lisa and Kerry . . . My mum still says to me even now, "Those girls . . . they'll lead you down the wrong path one day", and their mums say the same about me, 'cause I live down here . . . Funny that. If only they realized how much of the same goes on back home, right under their noses . . . literally. Ahhh, I can't wait to see them.'

Marly tried ringing Nick, her friend in the film company, when she got back to Chalk Farm. She was nervous, only because you can never really be sure of people and their promises, especially when you'd been slightly involved with them. Marly had met Nick when he'd directed a short film in Dublin and she'd been roped in as an assistant. He was an old-school thirty-something, typically English in his laid-back, detached manner, but redeemed by an equally English sick sense of humour, especially on the subject of his ex-wife, whom he affectionately referred to as the 'troll' or, on a bad day, that 'money-grabbing gnome'. He was, however, delighted to hear from Marly.

'How are you, Nicholas?'

'Oh, fine. Saw the ex crossing Fulham Road this morning in front of me. I tried to swerve but I fucking missed her. How are you, darling? Got here safe and sound, then?'

'Oh, yeah. It's been a laugh so far. The flat's great and all that. I'm going to come up and see you, though, if it's still all right.'

'No problem. I'm out tonight to some boring old git's birthday. I have to go 'cause I'm a creep and he wants a producer for his documentary. Why don't you come into the office on . . . say Tuesday. That old trout Nicky'll be there and she's still keen to get someone in full-time to order her avocado bagels at lunchtime and shuffle papers around. You're still on for it, aren't you, love?'

'God, yeah . . . I mean, it's just the sort of thing I'm looking for and –' She tried not to sound desperate.

'Oh, shut up!' He laughed. 'You're skint and unemployed and you'll take anything at the moment. Don't start all that media-girl small talk. There's enough of those silly witches around here already. Take the number and call me there first thing Tuesday.'

Marly was relieved.

'Fucking nice one,' said Lee, and Kate gave her a squeeze. 'Ahh, that's great,' she said in her vague, cloudy fashion.

They were all a bit jittery in a Saturday-night sort of way. The way that you feel nervous and uptight for no reason until you know exactly what you are doing.

'Well, I want to go to this thing with Paul,' said Kate. 'Where the hell is he? He said he'd ring and let us know about the guest list.'

'I promised Lisa and Kell we'd go to Pinacoladarada. They want to get right dressed up tonight 'cause they haven't been out in ages and they're right on the pull at the moment. Plus Trev Sovaine is doing a two-hour set and I love all the stuff he plays. I've got that *Restoration* II CD with his remix of 'Been Foolin'' by Wendy House.' She went to put it on in her bedroom.

Lisa and Kerry arrived in Kerry's mini at about seven.

'That fucking traffic was horrible. Hiya, darlings.' Kerry hugged Lee and Kate and smiled broadly at Marly. 'Oh, you've just moved in, haven't you? How're you finding scary old London? I tell you, I couldn't live here. It's so polluted and I get really bad asthma,' she said, lighting up a Rothman's. 'It's all right for the fortnightly drugs binge, though, innit, Lee?'

They shrieked with laughter together. Lisa came through the kitchen door having dragged both hers and Kelly's bulging overnight bags up the stairs.

'Those fucking stairs. Bit stingy on the width front, in't they?'

They sat and smoked some of Kate's skunk, while they waited for the Chinese they'd ordered. Kerry and Lisa fought for the shower; Kerry won.

'I shouldn't complain. She needs it more than I do, the dirty cow,' Lisa said in mock-bitchiness as they came back into the kitchen. 'So, what's happening tonight, then?'

Paul still wasn't back, so they decided that they'd go to meet Dani and Sheba up in DipStix, a pre-club bar in Soho, leaving a message for him to call them on Dani's mobile if he came up with any freebies.

When all five had finally emerged from the initial bathroom phase they relaxed a bit, taking time over clothes and make-up, the second stage, broken up by the odd line on the living-room table. Lee's room was a haemorrhage of clothes, shoes and accessories.

The old thrill of a build-up to a night out hadn't changed since the beginning of dance halls. Whatever the music or the scene, the routine was the same. The wondrous transformation of girls into their nocturnal forms, sometimes unrecognizable from their daytime selves, was a curious sight. Skin became glossy and iridescent, hair was coaxed into place with immaculate results, bodies sheathed in glittering fragments designed to grab attention and hold their own under nightclub lighting.

'COME ON AND REACH FOR ME –'

Lisa and Kerry sang along loudly out of tune and pranced around the flat in their underwear. Marly liked their unaffected way and how unaware they were of their remarkable looks.

It was the Paris collections for beginners. All over the city and beyond, the ghosts of girls and boys from every walk of life fled the confines of the day and made for the shady sparkle of clubland.

Rover came up at about half-nine with Lee's order and as she paid him the £60 for six Es, he stole sly glances at the girls in various stages of undress.

'Fuck me,' he accidentally said out loud.

'What?' said Lee, surprised.

'Oh, um, nothing. Have you got some papers I could have?'

'Yeah, in the kitchen.'

Lee expected him to take them on his way out. Instead, he came back into the living room and sat down on the sofa, deliberately near the coke chopped out on the blackness of a Chanel ad on the back cover of *Vogue*.

Kerry came into the room, ready apart from lipstick and shoes, and bent down for a line. She automatically offered a line to Rover, who said, 'Yes, please', without a moment's pause.

Lee was annoyed but said nothing. He'd probably want to go out with them now too.

Sure enough: 'So, what are you girls doing tonight, then?'

'Oh, just going out for a drink, probably,' answered Lee, quick as a flash.

'Yeah? Where's that. then? Up Soho, yeah? Oh, right. Nice. Yeah . . . I'll probably just sit in and chill tonight. Yeah, I been rushing around all day. I'll probably just put on some sounds, you know . . . Maybe check out the box . . .'

Lee's resolve was strong. She wasn't going to give in this time. This happened on a regular basis, especially when, curiously enough, Kerry was down. It was a long-running joke that Rover had a crush on her.

'I mean, I could always sort out my records or something . . .'

That did it. He was breaking her heart now.

'Well, why . . . why don't you . . .' Go on, it wouldn't be that bad. 'Why don't you come out with us?' Please say no, please.

'Oh, OK, blinding. I'll just nip downstairs and have a wash.'

He was gone in a waft of Geranium oil.

'*Lee!*' called Kerry. 'You've done it again, haven't you. Now I'm going to be stuck with him all night.'

'He'll be all right . . . As soon as he's stuck some drugs in his gob, he'll just wander off on his own.'

Paul still wasn't back when they left for town. They got the tube to Leicester Square and walked from there to the bar. The freak show of London on a Saturday night was in its first act. Loonies, smackheads at the end of their tether, Euro-tourists sleeping rough, smart-casual City boys pissed beyond belief, sleazy middle-aged singles strolling the streets on their own, hissing and tongue-clicking at girls walking by:

'Hello, pretty', 'Very nice', 'Where are you going?', 'Sexy bitch.' The gay Mafia buzzed around their hive of bars and cafés, all struggling to be the queen bee, the most stunning, the fittest, the hippest, the most entertaining. Their collective beauty was astonishing, a host of angel faces on perfect bodies.

The girls and Rover arrived at the bar at eleven. The throng spilled out on to the street. It was a serious affair, while the music was up-beat and frilly. One song sang of Neglect and Respect and how '*You want my poo-nani.*'

'You want my *what*?' said Rover, straining at the lyrics.

The pressure of maintaining cool among this crowd was tough. Everyone was drinking, downing their happy pills, all among friends, but hardly anyone smiled. The girls assessed one another like fillies in a paddock, sneering at the wrong shoes, the odd make-up or hair *faux pas* or weight problem. Marly felt a little apprehensive, while Lee and the others seemed perfectly at home. She dipped across the room, saying her hellos. Kate spotted Dani and Sheba at the bar and beckoned them over.

'Oliver hasn't turned up yet. He was supposed to meet me at ten,' fretted Dani. 'I hope he hasn't forgotten.'

'Look, there's that DJ, whatsername, Rachel Racket. I wonder if she's playing somewhere tonight.'

'I fucking hope not,' said Sheba bitchily.

'So, where do you work, then?' Marly asked Kerry, as she and Lisa brought the drinks over and sat down.

'In a fuck boring solicitors' office in Brackstead. I'm secretary to one of the partners. Really nice, isn't it, Lisa?' she said, raising her eyes skywards. 'Especially when you work for a perverted old goat who keeps telling you how sexy your bum is, and when you come in after a heavy weekend says things like, "Ooh, your boyfriend tiring you out, is he?"'

'Oh, he's horrible,' agreed Lisa. 'He looks like that little skinny one out of them *Carry On* films. You know, the one with the specs who's right into camping.'

They laughed and shared more stories about dodgy past employers. Marly told one about hers in France when she au-paired, who kept stealing her knickers out of her room and she'd find them in his bedside cabinet. Needless to say, she quitted in a hurry, but not before she lost twelve pairs. Lisa and Kerry screamed in horror, 'The dirty old frog.'

Dani suddenly fixed her look on a crowd coming through the door. It was her long-awaited 'date', Oliver, and his entourage of hangers-on and a posse of beautiful babes. He stayed at the bar for about ten minutes before heading through the crowd in their direction. Dani made as if to stand up and greet him, but he dodged tables and went straight past her to the men's. She felt foolish and exposed. Marly felt like saying 'Who cares?' but she didn't think it would help. No one had noticed the 'blank', as Dani viewed it, but she was mortified and lit a fag with shaking hands. Five minutes later, however, he came out and rushed up to her, grabbing her from behind, and gave her a big hug. Her forgiveness was instant. His eyes were sparkling as he brushed a few specks of powder from his upper lip, while his companion stood silent, looking a little bored.

'Hiya, Ol. What are you up to?' Dani beamed up at him, with a perfect matt-beige smile.

'Heading down to my do at Pinacoladarada. Not for long, though. Zak's got some nice shit, so we'll probably go back to mine later. What about you?'

'I dunno,' she said, hoping he would ask her too. 'See what happens.'

'Well, do you want me to put you lot down? It's pretty full, but I'll manage it. Girls only, mind. How many?'

He gave her his address for later if they wanted to 'pop by, have a drink, whatever', then he was off, taking his gaggle with him, chattering and bubbling.

'Oliver's mate was wisting at you, Marly,' said Kate.

'No, he wasn't. He was coked off his face.'

'He was *what* at you?' asked Dani suspiciously.

'Wisting . . . We made it up in France. You know, when a bloke looks at you. He was really fit as well.'

'Well, a look's probably all I'll get tonight,' Marly said gloomily.

Paul phoned them about half-twelve on the mobile as they walked to the club.

'I'm still at my mate Adam's in Brixton. I think we're going up the Temple, but I can only get in with him – his mate's doing a live PA. If you lot want to come, you'll have to meet us first.'

'Oh, well. We'll leave it, then. Cheers anyway,' said Kate and rang off. 'That's that, then. We might as well go to this thing now we're here.'

Marly was disappointed. She'd been looking forward to going out with Paul and to meeting his friends. He had an easy way about him, along with the constant promise of fun. She cast him from her mind as Rover suddenly put his hand on her back while they crossed the busy road.

'Don't you know your Green Cross Code?'

Marly hid her sigh and raised a smile.

BB sat in his room in his mum's and dad's Shepherd's

Bush semi, listening to a deep-throated, spiralling cacophony of death knells and hissing percussion called 'Shadow Puppet', by a mysterious Belgian count who called himself Ropey. He was too skint to go to the techno night in Bow, where Wiz and Virgil had gone. Just as well, he told himself. He felt angry and upset at their nonchalant attitude over the previous night's disaster. H had a bit of a chill after being out in the cold all night, so he was staying in for once with his girlfriend, who was looking after him. Barry and Colin had apparently gone AWOL. Their mums both said they hadn't seen them since Thursday and would appreciate a phone call if BB did. Kraftwerk's 'Computerworld' played softly on CD. Still his all-time favourite.

BB felt useless sitting there. He couldn't even get up the enthusiasm to fool about on his keyboards and come up with something for the techno track. They had planned to send it to a bloke Virgil knew in Amsterdam who was 'very much interested in you English boys and your underground techno scene'. He decided to go out for a wander. He wanted to think about his next move. There were more opportunities for his crusade than ever on a Saturday night. He needed inspiration. With £3 in his pocket, enough for a packet of ten and a couple of bus fares, he set off.

They stopped before they reached the vast queue, stretching along High Holborn, swallowing their pills in case they were searched. Rover had received a message from a customer on his pager and went off to phone him. He'd probably have to go back home, he said, and sort out a couple of ounces for this bloke. He was sorry to leave them and all that . . .

'Oh, no, don't worry. Next time, eh?' said Lee a little too quickly.

They got in after a few moments' hassle and nail-biting and Lee getting arsy with the bouncer.

'Yeah, if you'd like to actually use your reading skills, you might have a better chance of actually seeing the names. Yeah, that's it, "Oliver + 2 and Dani + 2". Well done, mate.'

The bouncer watched her go in with yobby contempt. Gleaming pixie girls wasted their youth and beauty on these fat burly grizzlies, always mindful that the bums could come in handy for future nights out.

The lights flashed green and blue as they went into the main hall. The *Saturday Night Fever* layout was impressive, with mirrored columns and a flashing dance floor. Scarily gorgeous trannies towered over small boys, choking them as they danced with their ostrich boas. They saw Oliver at a table in the bar, sitting with some babes and the keyboard player from a well-known eighties pop group, once a household name, now a coky has-been trying to break into acting. Dani made a quick trip to the loos to check in the mirror that everything was as it should be before going over casually with Sheba. Kate and Marly went to check out the dance floor, while the others went to the bar to get a round of beers.

'Three fucking quid, you're having a laugh.'

Lee said it every time, knowing full well the price of drinks there. But, as she said, you had to make a point.

The dance floor wasn't quite full enough to dance comfortably and they all sat down with Oliver's crowd, who were wide-eyed with the enthusiasm that coke inspires in even the greatest dullards.

'I can't see the point of doing coke all night in a club. It's one thing doing it early on, you know, just to get you going, but it wears off so quickly and you're running into those dodgy loos all the time, getting backache bending over the bog-roll holder. What a waste of money,' whispered Kate.

Sheba was telling one of Oliver's babe entourage about her acting. 'Well, he did promise me a part in his new video, you know, the one he's directing for that American band who are supposed to be like Nirvana. I'm hopeless with names, but apparently their lyrics are really good. You know, really intelligent. Anyway, I'm apparently going to play the girl lying on the slab at the morgue with, like, just a pair of rubber gloves on and an apron. You know, to sort of signify the enslavement and murder of women by men within the home and all that. Anyway, I saw him last week when he came back to my flat and he seemed really into it and we had a great time. You know, smoking about half an ounce between us. God, I was really fucked. Anyway, then he left, after we'd finished that and said he'd call. So, fingers crossed –'

The music became more prominent in Marly's mind

now. She listened to it intently as her body went through a series of changes. The air became thicker as she breathed in. She looked around aimlessly at the dark, glossy interior. She wondered what to do with herself. She didn't feel like talking any more. These pills were strong. They took hold of her and she felt an invasion of the senses. She was powerless against it.

'You've just got to let it happen. If you don't resist, you'll have no problems.' She'd been told that the very first time she'd taken E. She stood up and made for the next room, where the dance floor was filling up, and stood and watched as one person after the next gave up to the music.

'I Know a Place', a smooth, happy singsong tune, came on and she danced along with the room. Kate and Sheba joined her. She spotted Lee on the other side with her mates. They were smiling and fooling about, Lee was doing silly dances, making fun of strangers and trying to get them to join in. She looked down and fixed her eyes on the lights on the dance floor. Someone had joined them. She looked up into the lights and couldn't make out his face properly, her vision flickering with the strobes.

'I think Rover's been keeping these pills in a bag with his acid,' Kate mumbled, as she too looked as wrecked as Marly felt.

Marly looked back at the figure next to them. He smiled at her. It was Oliver's friend from the bar. They danced along on the spot, until her mind clouded over and she forgot where she was. She understood now why the music was so simple and childish. Each track had a train of rhythm you could climb on to until the drugs died away. All the positive sensations were here, thriving on the music with its transparent soul. High times without any depths.

'TAKE ME BACK TO LOVE, TAKE ME BACK TO LOVE –'

She went with it, feeling the warmth being here with Kate, and looked at the boy with affection simply because he was close by. She knew nothing about him, except that he was giving off a nice vibe. There was no other word for it.

She said to Kate that she was going off for another drink. Her heart was beating fast as she joined the table and sat there, detached from the chattering girls, listening when her ears would let her. The boy on the dance floor joined her a few minutes later. He said hello and sat down and offered her a cigarette. She couldn't light it, so he took it from her and gave her his in return. He had green eyes which were like ice in the igloo of UV and his pupils were large pools of brown. She thought he looked like something exotic sitting there. He had a languid, comfortable air as if he'd always had an easy ride in life.

His name was Sean and he knew Oliver from when they'd worked in the same studio years ago. They sat and talked nonsense about random things – TV shows, one-night stands, music, Oliver's drug habit, the girls sitting at the table and how Sean couldn't stand them, as, the first thing they always asked was what did he do for a living, sniffing out his usefulness as a 'new friend'. He made her laugh with a story about some mates of his up north out tripping one night in the local park. They hadn't realized there was an open-air theatre there with a performance of The Wizard of Oz in progress and how they came across the Lion, the Tin Man and the Scarecrow having a sly smoke under a tree in the interval.

'One jumped in a bush and hid and the other went up and had a fag with them. They didn't find out till they got home there'd been a play on.'

Oliver stood up to leave. Sean looked at his watch and asked if she was coming back to the flat with them.

'I can't really. All my friends are here. I think we're going to stay till the end.'

'Come round later, then.' He gave her the address.

Dani was leaving too in Oliver's wake, fighting as hard as she could against all the gorgeous creatures more at home in the 'big league' than she. Marly gave her credit for trying.

The club was into its full on stage now. Everywhere there were huge eyes, water swiggers, make-up retouches in the toilets, sweat, sticky hair, tops coming off. The DJ was up there on his pedestal, tripping, Eing and staring at the three blue dolphins on the label of the twelve-inch on the decks. The grooves spun out-wards into infinity and he couldn't take his eyes off them. A strange girl stood next to the box, drawing pic-tures on a pad of paper, as if she was trying to capture what he was playing.

Marly fell back into the music as she joined her friends, who were in the middle of the heaving throng. Her trance lasted longer than the last. Only when a stray crusty started playing the bongos in the corner did the pit-pat wake her from her reverie. She stared, unblinking, at the mass of wet skin around her, all the bodies had an eerie latex look, reflecting the uniform butterscotch tans. She couldn't take her eyes off a transvestite's rear that wiggled nearby. She wondered if any of the blokes she knew would look like that in hotpants. Now Kate was trying to tell her about some Germans who'd been chatting her up at the bar.

'I just can't get on with them. "Ah, ya, London iss so groovy, I like very much ze Englissh girls." God, and all their culture's so harsh and weird, just like them. Not like the Irish, are they?'

'Oh, yeah,' Marly replied with difficulty – her mouth was so dry, 'We've got the fucking Cranberries. Great.' She stumbled off to the bar.

In the shadows of an alley sandwiched between Burger Delight and Tempo hi-fi shop stood BB. His eyes were temporarily blinded by a flash of car headlights turning down the small road. He dropped his fag and stepped behind a big plastic wheelie bin. Back in darkness he drew his windcheater around him and stared across the road.

The small but still buzzing queue was lit up by the strip lights of a nearby boutique, shining on the expectant, wasted faces, which he suddenly had an uncontrollable urge to smash in. What was it about them and their scene that so disturbed him? Was it the fact that he couldn't handle the buoyant, lilting happiness of it all? Or that everyone had to look like a fucking mannequin to feel at home?

BB secretly knew he could never look right in that gear, being a portly fifteen stone (he'd always been a chubby child), with a pasty complexion marred by a slight skin complaint, the result of a junk-food diet and too many drugs at an early age. Even his name was all wrong. Born Bernard Bolton, he knew it would do him no favours to keep it that way.

He looked at his watch. It was just after three. The queue was easing off now and the bouncers kept leaving their posts to nip off for sly joints or to chat up girls on the stairs. BB stepped out of the gloom and slowly walked towards the ropes. He slipped past the sole remaining bouncer with ease and sneaked down the stairs. With his murky grey-green hood over his head, eyes downcast, he almost blended in with the mock-breezeblock walls and nearly fell over a gaggle of girls on their way out.

'Oh, God, sorry,' said the first in a soft Irish accent.

'Kate, where do we get a cab from?' They breezed past him and were gone.

Downstairs a blast of heat smacked him in the face as he approached the main room and the sound of piano chords coming from the dance floor which he hadn't heard for years but now was strangely drawn towards. A few stray clubbers sitting hugging themselves and chatting on a couch at the entrance stared at him as if he were an alien. He glanced back and blushed, hurrying on inside. What was he doing here?

The track playing inside reached its climax and he stepped through the doors as the crowd rushed with the music. He stood on the fringes and watched. Someone asked him for a cigarette as he took out his box. He was stunned that anyone had noticed him. The boy took his last cigarette as he stood there, tongue-tied.

'Ah, cheers, mate. You saved my life. Here you go.' He winked, pressed half a white pill in BB's hand and danced off.

BB swallowed it, feeling strangely liberated, and moved closer to the throbbing speakers.

Outside, the girls hailed a black cab to go to Oliver's. Marly shivered uncontrollably as the cold hit her. Lee, Kerry and Lisa looked like ghouls in the stark lights. They'd got hold of another couple of pills inside and split them and were now gurning ever so slightly, but still managing to just about hold it together.

'Where're we going?' they must have asked three times, then all giggled when told the answer.

'Who the fuck is Oliver? Oh, yeah, *him*. The sex fiend.' They all cracked up laughing.

'Don't mention that in front of him,' Kate admonished them. 'Dani's trying to pull him.'

'Well, she'd better get herself down fucking King's Cross, then,' said Lee as they cracked up again.

*

Marly had never seen a flat like it. It was straight out of *The Bitch*. A flashy, expensive living room with black leather sofas on a white-tiled 'Mediterranean feel' floor, Goan wall-hangings and Japanese erotic sculptures. Framed Herb Ritts photos on the walls. There was a turquoise breakfast counter with some Philippe Starck stools in the kitchen, a fifties-style leopard-skin cocktail bar in the corner of the room, stocked with kitsch knick-knacks, and in the middle of the lounge a huge, low, glass coffee table with spiky wrought-iron coils rising out of the middle.

The crowd sitting in the living room were watching an American made-for-TV movie called *The Seeds of Hate*, laughing at all the corny lines: 'I'm not the linen, you know. You can't just change me when you like,' said Ricardo Montalbain with a smouldering look as he undid his trousers.

They were all fucked in one way or another. A couple of models sat by the coffee table snorting huge lines of coke into their perfect noses, while a crowd of heavy-duty smokers sat on the small terrace balcony among Oliver's plants.

'No flicking ash or butts in my babies, please,' shouted Oliver from the kitchen. He was standing at the counter with his babe for that week making tall jugs of Margaritas.

The place was très 'Swinging London' – hip, groovy and designed for entertaining. Marly heard one of the beautiful boys sitting on the couch with Dani and

Sheba say, 'Ollie tries to spend only six months of the year here in London and the rest in Tasmania or Mexico, just chilling out.'

A bedroom door opened and Sean popped his head out. He saw her and beckoned her and Kate over. They went in. The room had a huge emperor-sized bed covered with a black and red Samurai print cover. Sean patted the bed and offered them a spliff going round.

'I fancy some more drugs,' he said.

'I got some nice doves if you want,' said an effeminate male model standing over by the window, looking up at the stars with an equally gorgeous girl.

'Yeah, cheers, mate. Um . . . Give us three if you got them.' Sean gave him some cash and took one with a swig of fruit punch.

'Do you two want one?' he asked the girls.

Marly paused. She was feeling a bit stagnant and didn't want to go home yet. 'Yeah, OK. Thanks very much.' She swallowed hers with a wince. Kate declined, yawning. Marly was a bit annoyed that Kate would probably want to crash out soon, but said nothing.

A heavily made-up, beautifully dressed Japanese girl came out of the *en-suite* bathroom and fell back on to the bed with a sigh. 'Everyone's so boring here. I wanna go to Raid, but no one come with me. I just took another pill and I wanna dance.'

Sean raised his eyes at Marly. 'Just relax, Yosh. There's music here. You can start the dancing. Go on, show us what you can do,' he said good-naturedly.

'Oh, you shut up. You so old and boring, you like my grandfather. What are you doing with him? she turned and asked Marly, her eyes barely focusing.

Marly laughed. 'He's supposed to be showing me a good time,' she answered cheekily.

'Oh, you know straight men are sooo *anal*. All my friends for clubbing are gay, you know. They sooo fun and lot of life and look good all the time and they so clean too. You know, even my cat, he gay. No, he is. He gay and he only like guys who come to my house who are gay too. Sean, if you come to my house, my cat gonna pee on you. No, really, he pee on my landlord, and my brother, he came over for holiday from Japan and he pee on him too.'

Sean went on the decks in Oliver's bedroom for a while and Yoshika, Marly and Kate danced. Lee came in after a bit, all excited and very blitzed, to tell them there was a minor soap star in the other room and he was dishing out the Charlie like nobody's business. Yoshika barged straight past her when she heard this and plumped herself down next to him.

The main room was a menagerie of wackos, or at least people doing their best to resemble something strange and exotic. Most of the girls were beautiful and most of the boys striking. Much of the illusion was created by their outfits and polished exteriors, which can only be achieved by the very rich.

Kerry and Lisa were sitting with a merry-looking imp of a bloke called Chester. He must have been pushing forty and was gleefully chopping out lines and handing them around. He was, Sean told Marly as they sat together on the high stools by the bar, a doctor who had been struck off, but he still made use of his pharmaceutical skills by mixing his own drugs at home and trying them out on his friends. The room was a surgery to him, full of drug casualties in need of a diagnosis.

They watched him at 'work': 'Come on. You've been on that buzz long enough. I think you need a line of coke.' 'No, no, don't worry. I've got some valium somewhere . . . .' 'Well, of course you won't sleep. It's crystal meth. Just take a couple of sleeping pills. You'll be fine.' His well-spoken voice cut through the room like a steely blade, but no one seemed to care where anyone was from here. Drugs made just about anyone and anything acceptable. Just about.

Chester came over, got a drink and stood with Marly and Sean for a while.

'Why, she's lovely,' he said to Sean looking Marly up and down with wide, approving eyes. 'I do love the Irish. So passionate. Do you want a line, darling?'

She liked talking to him, even just for novelty value. His wit was refreshing after so much slurry rambling. It made her realize that he had a control over his drug habit that many of the people here lacked. Drugs controlled them, but this seemed to be what they were after. Or perhaps, after years of popping pills, Chester was just a little more immune than the rest.

Sheba had crashed out on the floor, her hair lying in

a pile of coke on a mirror. Oliver came out of the bed-room and clocked it.

'God, there's a fucking babe in my Chaz.'

Sean and Marly went to sit on the balcony as her E was coming up and she was feeling rushy and hot. Two men were in the bamboo seats. Dante, 'as in Dante's *Inferno*', as he introduced himself, was clad in leather trousers and Cuban-heeled boots, with a zebra-pat-terned waistcoat over a tanned bare chest. The thought of this bloke walking down the street in Ballykill, her home town, made her laugh, as he would, without a doubt, proverbially – no, literally – get the shit kicked out of him. He and his friend, Marcus, were talking about their respective music careers.

'So I said to Rod that I loved the new "Scoundrel of Rock" image. I mean the guy is maturing gracefully. He knows what he likes. He's got fabulous PR people around him. That *Unplugged* was the best thing he ever could have done. You know, at his time of life, it's hard to make the right decision. You turn the wrong thing down, it could be your last,' he said sagely.

'Yeah, and you should know, mate,' said Sean under his breath. Marly elbowed him in the ribs. 'So, how was the tour with Blub?' he asked Marcus.

'Oh, sure . . . fine,' Marcus replied dismissively.

'Really? I heard things got a bit nasty.' Dante was fishing.

'Nothing of the sort, mate. We just, er, agreed to differ on a few matters, that's all.' Marcus shifted uncomfortably.

'Oh, right. I heard . . . I mean, I'm sure it's just music-biz back-stabbing, but, like, I heard that you woke up one morning and they'd all checked out of the hotel without you and that they'd left a plastic bag full of shit outside your door and a note saying –'

'Yeah,' Marcus butted in, 'well, if you're gonna believe idle gossip . . . Is there any more of that Charlie going?' He got up sharply and went inside.

Kate came out just then to say that they were leaving. Lee had almost had a fight with Yoshika over the 'actor' and Kerry didn't feel well.

'Do you want to get a cap with us or . . .' She looked at Sean.

'I'm just going to get a drink,' said Sean, tactfully withdrawing. 'If you want to stay, I'll see you home,' he added before he left.

'So?' beamed Kate. 'What's the story?'

'No story yet. I don't know. I don't know him. Do you think he's, you know, all right?'

'Well, he seems really nice. Stay and have a chat with him and if you're not keen just get a cab later. I hate to leave you, but I'm zonked. Have you got money? All right then. Be good.' She kissed Marly on the cheek and went in to drag Lee away from her ruck.

Sean came back with the drinks. 'I could do with listening to some decent music. Do you want to go inside? Or we could split and go to mine. My flatmate's probably back by now. He'll be up with some mates. It'll be a bit more sane than this fucking place.'

Marly felt like taking a chance. 'OK. Let's go.'

They said their goodbyes. Dani and Sheba were still sitting on the couch, looking pissed off at the lack of attention they were getting from Oliver and the soap star, the only two men in the room who held any interest for them (the rest being gay or Marcus and Dante). They both made a big show of Marly leaving with Sean, winking and putting their thumbs up, and said they'd speak to her soon.

The room seethed and swayed before BB's eyes, becoming a pleasurable sight. These birds were a bit of all right. Why didn't you ever get girls like that down the places he went to? It really was like a nice package hol in Tenerife. All these birds with their kit off . . .

The barriers set up in his mind against the music, the fashions, the whole scene started to slip down as his feet began moving against his will. He couldn't help himself as Colourblind's skyscraping anthem came raging on to the dance floor:

'THERE'S NOTHING BETTER . . .

NOTHING BETTER –'

Unknowingly BB had put on the red shoes and he was under their spell. Slowly he started to dance.

Back at Sean's they found his flatmate on his way to bed. He was off the drugs, he said, and so had drunk far too much and was either going to pass out or be sick and much preferred the first option. He said hello and goodbye very politely to Marly, though, and shut the bedroom door with a groan.

Sean put Cabaret Voltaire on and made them some tea. They sat on the couch and he put his arm around her. He gave her a secure feeling among all the narcotic confusion of the night.

At the age of thirty-one, he'd been around. His tales were about his early days in Manchester. Dodgy connections and law-breaking mates, some of whom were now inside, robberies gone wrong, tricks played on the police, scams pulled, early bands, his punk phase and mod days. Best of all, Sean kept his sense of humour on drugs. He seemed a little shy with Marly now they were alone, not once suggesting they move to the bedroom, but content to take her hand and hold it between his. His energy was spent on talking. It seemed he had none left for anything else.

He decided to take some more E and Marly agreed, wanting to be on the same level as him, but also feeling like she could carry on all day. They brought a duvet out from the bedroom and curled up and talked about the music they were listening to. No sex. She had to admit she was a little disappointed. Those celebrated side-effects of E, it was all true. She tried to ignore it.

The time ran on like a river. They watched the sky change into an afternoon gold and went down to a pub by the canal in Maida Vale. She borrowed some sunglasses and sat outside while Sean went to get some drinks. They both drank one after another, with raging thirsts. Marly leant back and looked at him intently through Sean's black shades. In the daylight he did

look older, but the tiny lines barely visible around his eyes, probably due more to drug taking than anything else, gave his face a soft anxious air.

'What are you going to do for work?' he asked her, and she explained.

'You want to watch that media crowd. They'll eat you up. They're in a business which you can't define and you never know what's round the corner. They're all a bit desperate. It's just the same as the music scene. That's why I have as little as possible to do with it now. I only want to know those people second-hand.'

Here goes, thought Marly. 'Well, what are you up to at the moment, then?' She hoped it sounded casual.

'Ah, a few bits and pieces. Me and my mate have got a mail-order thing. Buying and selling records to collectors. Abroad mainly. That's what keeps me going. Then there's this bloke I know from when I was living in the States who's connected to this big label. He gets me to keep an eye open for new talent and do a bit of writing and producing with them, if the need arises, which it usually does. It's a joke really, but I get a bit of a weekly wage for it. I'm probably just a tax-loss project, but they might as well spend their money here in Europe. Well, that's showbiz.'

They sat there till it started getting cold and went back to watch a film. Neither of them was hungry, but Marly asked if she could have a shower and ransacked the basket of hotel bath-gels and shampoos. The hot water made her head rush. It felt good and straightened out her thoughts a little. She felt slightly unreal, being in a stranger's flat two days after arriving in London, but it was exciting all the same.

She came back into the room where Sean sat on the floor, nodding his head, lost in music. She flopped on to the couch and closed her eyes. She could feel her own body acutely. Each nerve bristled with an electric charge. She tried to remember how her body felt when she was sixteen and wondered if she was the same person.

Seven

BB felt ashamed as he picked up the phone. It was six o'clock Sunday evening and he'd been woken up by his mum saying Wiz wanted to talk to him.

'All right, mate?' came Wiz's adenoidal whine. 'What d'you get up to last night, then?'

'Ummm . . . Not much, mate. You know, just sat in and mucked about with some music,' lied BB. 'Went to bed pretty early and that.'

'You missed some blinding night, Guv. I got hold of some nice pink champagne from some geezer down that club in Bow. Haven't been to kip yet. So, what d'you lay down last night, music-wise? Anything decent?'

'Um, no, no,' panicked BB. 'Nothing worth doing anything with. You know, just a bit of a laugh.'

BB didn't want Wiz sniffing around and, God forbid, finding out that after the club he'd floated home and, inspired by the tunes of the night, laid down a fully fledged strings and all happy handbag tune. He couldn't believe it himself and the memory haunted him like a horrible grasping fiend.

'So, what are you doing tonight? Are we going to have a meeting or what? Me and Virg come up with some blinding ideas for them ponces, once we actually get hold of some, that is. We thought, like, we could hold them down, get their threads off and make 'em put on some fucking 'orrible shell suits and take pictures and send them round to all them mags or even to their mates and . . .'

Wiz droned on and BB gradually came to his senses. What had he done? He'd better just put the whole episode out of his mind and get back to business. He had to finish what he'd started.

Col and Baz thought it time to make amends with BB. They decided to go round as a surprise with a peace offering of a couple of ready-rolled and a few beers.

'You go first,' said Baz, pushing Col ahead as they approached his driveway.

'Fuck off, it was your idea.'

'Look, this is stupid. I mean, what's the worst he can do?'

'I don't know. I mean, he's fucking serious about all this stuff. It's everything to him. He lives it, he really does.'

'I wish I had something I felt that, you know, passionate about,' mumbled Baz.

They went round the back way, as was the ritual when there was no car in the drive, signifying that BB's parents had gone out.

Inside BB sat in front of his keyboards, his AKAI S1100 sampler and Atari 1040 computer, trying to clear his mind and get on with his original ideas for the track for their Dutch techno contact. For some reason he couldn't get the tunes of the previous night out of his head.

Why were those fucking dodgy gospel vocals still pounding around his head? They were just so . . . catchy. He glanced down at the DAT lying on the table, the product of last night's madness. He picked it up and looked at it with contempt, then slowly, against his will, put it into his machine. The track started with a tinkle of snowfall sounds on synths, sampled from GrandMaster Flash 'White Lines', then a bass travelling up and down to introduce the beat, which had layers of various other percussion on top, all building up bar after bar to a crescendo of beautiful fluid lines with peaks of strings barely discernible in the background. He's sampled a vocal from an old early disco compilation album of his mum's and that added the necessary camp spiciness. As he listened to it, he felt strangely uplifted and tried to ignore the fact that his foot was tapping.

Colin and Barry were approaching his bedroom window and just about to tap on it when they both stopped in their tracks.

'What the fuck's that?'

They listened in disbelief and looked at one another pale-faced. It couldn't be true, it couldn't be BB listening to this. It was as if they had just heard their mum and dad shagging. They were wholly embarrassed, dumbfounded beyond belief. Speechless, they tiptoed away into the autumn dusk.

Marly called Nick on Tuesday morning and he said to come as soon as she was ready. They'd meet with Nicky, her fingers-crossed boss-to-be, and then have a boozy lunch somewhere. Nicky was a hard-nosed divorcée producer who was an expert in the art of schmoozing and getting what she wanted out of people, especially men and especially the gruff, no-nonsense type who worked on the technical side of film and TV. They melted under her professional pandering. One look at her honey-blonde hair, her ruby lips and, if they were lucky, her tanned peachy cleavage, and they'd agree to any salary, any hours and any deal. She was pushing forty but still cut it on the temptress front, being one of those lucky 'girls' who looked roughly the same as they had at eighteen, especially in the dim pastel office lighting she insisted on. She was, however, said Nick, a fair employer, paid you well and was generous with the freebies.

Nicky was busy when Marly came in, so she waited in reception under the watchful gaze of two pretty vultures in reception.

'You can go up now.'

They watched her walk to the lift, then went back to their *Cosmo*s and stryofoam cappuccinos.

Nick greeted her with a big kiss on the lips, which Marly tried to dodge. He smoothed her hair, picked a speck of fluff off her black jumper and led her by the hand into Nicky's office.

'Darling, this is Marly. She's going to be your lifesaver, I just know it. I can certainly vouch for her mouth to mouth.' He sniggered as he shut the door.

Nicky raised her eyes. 'God, you haven't slept with him too, have you? There should be a society in his name.'

'Oh, no, I just –' began Marly, worried Nicky might think she was a bimbo.

'Don't worry, darling. I know it's just his sick mind. He can't meet a pretty girl without at least trying. Now let me tell you what I'm looking for . . .'

'So, how was it for you, darling? Did she give you the one about "I'm tough but fair, I expect a lot but I give a lot in return"' asked Nick on the way to lunch, when Nicky had finally let her go at half-three. 'You've been in there ages.'

'She's all right. I don't know what you were talking

about. Knowing you, she probably turned you down. That's your problem with her,' teased Marly.

'Did she tell you . . . the old hoofer. I'll kill her.'

Marly got back at seven, a little worse for wear after the three bottles of wine they'd shared at lunch and a quick stop-off at Nick's mate's place in Wardour Street where they sat for an hour or so smoking joints with the friend, who was a fifty-something fat, jovial camera-man who told them stories about his last shoot, where he'd had the trying task of softening the lens on the leading lady, an extremely famous English star who caused endless problems on the shoot by having to be dragged out of the local every lunchtime after more than a few G&Ts.

'Well, how old is she exactly?' asked Nick.

'Let's just say she should be sampling the delights of free London Transport any day.'

Kate and Lee were expecting her and excited to hear her news.

'So, it sounds like you're in. Nice one. I don't know, you fucking paddies, you come over here with your Terry Wogans and your Henry fucking Kellys and you steal our jobs . . . I fancy a line to wake me up.'

Lee went off into her bedroom and came back a few minutes later, a little brighter.

'Who's coming to this thing tonight, then?'

'What is it?' asked Kate.

'Some night at Cramp called "Keep You Regular". It's that Restoration crowd that's organizing it.

Philippe's going and he said if we meet with him we can get in for half price. That's only four quid.'

'I'm knackered,' said Marly. 'Oh, were there any messages for me?' she asked, casually but hopefully.

'Oh, yeah, some bloke,' said Kate, racking her brains. Marly's heart gave a little twist.

'Umm . . . He had an Irish accent, um . . . Tony, that's it. He left a number.'

'Oh, yeah, and your mum called about six. She said she'd ring back tomorrow,' shouted Lee from the other room.

'So, what about it, girls? Go on, it'll be a laugh.'

Why not, Marly thought. She'd expected Sean to call and had that agitated feeling that comes of waiting for those first signs. She cringed at the thought that she was so bothered and tried to put it out of her mind. Sean certainly hadn't pushed her to stay on Sunday night, and she'd ended getting a cab home at about midnight, when he started yawning. She was feeling extra paranoid today, probably due to the post-E 'trauma', as Lee put it.

'What time is this thing on till?' 'I've got to go in tomorrow for a bit of a trial day.'

'Probably about two or three. Look, I've got to be up at half-eight too, you know,' Lee said a bit testily, implying Marly was a lightweight.

Paul came in a little later, from a hard day's painting walls in his mate's shop.

'What's for tea, mother?' He hugged Kate round the waist.

'Oh, God, you stink of turps. Go and have a bath, my lad, and I might think of doing you a nice bit of tripe.'

'What are you doing tonight, then?' he said, his head in the fridge.

'Well, I want to go out dancing, but these boring old slags won't come,' moaned Lee, draining her teacup, picking out leaves and pressing them on the table in a pattern. 'What about you?'

'I'm supposed to meet this bloke tonight for a pint and see if he still wants to go ahead with this studio. He said he ran one in the States this summer and reckons he can sort out something over here really cheap.'

'Didn't you say your new bloke was in America doing something musicy?' Kate asked Marly.

Paul looked up from the fridge and paused for just a second. 'Oh . . . What's all this? Have you got yourself a boyfriend? Didn't waste your time, did you?' he said, a little bitchily.

'Paul! Don't be so rude.' Lee and Kate looked at one another, surprised. This wasn't like him.

'It's a joke. For fuck's sake. Look, I didn't mean it like that, Marly.'

She laughed good-naturedly. Lee and Kate weren't convinced.

'I really can't go. I've got to do some bloody accounts for the boss. They were due in last week,' said Kate apologetically.

'All right, what's your excuse?' Lee stared at Marly with menace.

'OK, I'll come. Is it dressy?'

'Depends what you call dressy.'

'Do you think it's all right to bring someone? I was going to ask Tony, my brother's mate. I promised I'd invite him out.'

Marly already had the beginnings of a hangover and her body felt exhausted from the weekend, but she was determined to enjoy herself. They had endless trouble on the door because the supercilious, prickly trannie on the door disapproved of Tony's outfit. It took Lee and Philippe a great deal of sucking up before they could persuade 'her' to let him in. Marly heard Philippe bitching on the way downstairs about Tony.

'Who is that guy? He dresses like our gardener in Brazil.'

The place was packed by the time they got there and the dance floor was heaving with a mixed crowd. She wished Lee had said exactly how glamorous it was going to be. PVC mock-croc dresses, chiffon bustiers, snakeskin pencil skirts, Maraboa bras, tight satin pants, Blumarine, Vivienne Westood, Liza Bruce, D&G, Anna Sui, Jimmy Choo, Martine Sitbon and Joseph – all the names for those who could afford it or, if they couldn't, found the money somehow. She had wondered how Lee found the cash for her clothes and drugs, and realized she was in a desperate race to keep up with all this. She loved to feel good and this was the way to her heart. She hardly ate and had no other real expenses as her rent was paid by the housing. Marly figured her weekly income must be around £160 and practically all of that went on pills and clothes.

She and Lee went to the bar and came back with some warm beers. They went off to explore, leaving Tony and Philippe to, in Philippe's words, 'Get, how you say, aquatic with one another.' They went up to a balcony to watch the dancing and for Lee to do a line.

'Don't you want one?' she asked Marly, frowning at the burning sensation in her sinuses.

'No, I'm all right for the moment.'

'Oh, go on, for fuck's sake. You'll fall asleep if you don't.' Down on the dance floor were hundreds of writhing bodies, all urgent in their devotion to the moment. Whatever stage they had reached, it made no difference, they'd all peak in the end and then go home, recover and do it all over again the next night, the next week or the next month. The only real distinctions lay in the sizes of ther incomes, the confinements of their jobs or their capacity for drug taking.

Marly looked over to the table and saw, to her surprise, that Tony and Philippe were getting on famously.

'Come on. Let's go down to the others.'

Philippe was roaring with laughter as they sat down.

'Oh, you know, I love Irish boys – Boyzone, Larry from U2, that 'unky one from D-Ream. They're sooo saucy-looking, like big, strong farmer's boys.'

'Oh, stop being such a slag, Phil,' said Lee, annoyed. 'I tell you it's queens like you who give gay men a bad name. Look, Tony's going to think you're all sex fiends.'

'Well, I have been known,' replied Philippe camply.

'The thing that gets me,' began Tony, 'and don't take offence now, is why sex has to be your main identity tag. I mean, I've sat and chatted with you and it's been a great laugh and we haven't once mentioned what either of us gets up to in bed. So why do you put on a face like that. I'm telling you, that's what rubs gay bashers up the wrong way.'

'But, baby, that's exactly whad I wanna do.'

The two men looked at one another and burst out laughing.

'Come on, Marl. Leave them to bond. I just saw that Oliver over by the waltzer.' She pointed to a fairground ride in the corner, set up as a bar with the cabins as booths for people to sit down and have a drink in.

Marly felt ill as she approached his group, thinking that Sean might be there. She wished she hadn't done that coke. It was making her extra-tense and she couldn't think what to say.

There was no sign of Sean as they sat down, and Lee started her cheeky banter, monopolizing Oliver and his pop-star mate, much to the other girls' chagrin.

'Yeah, I always wanted to be in a band. I've written some songs. The best one's called "Silk Slut". It's about my heady life as a member of the glitterati.'

Marly sat there watching Tony on the dance floor looking like Philippe had slipped him something. She was bored and wasn't interested in the small talk around the table. The pop star seemed to find Lee hilarious.

'I've just finished this song, but the band don't want to record it. They think it's too raw and hard for our image. I'll give it to you if you like.' He leaned over lechily.

'Yeah, thanks, but I think your band are shit actually.'

Oliver laughed uproariously. 'Oh, I like this one. She's got balls.'

Marly had had enough. She went over to Tony and tried to ask him if he wanted to go home. His eyes were wide and sunken, but he was enjoying his E immensely, surrounded by beautiful 'women'. She wondered if he realized. He'd be there for hours. She was just contemplating getting a cab on her own when someone put a hand on her shoulder. She jumped. It was Sean, standing there with one of the girls from Oliver's flat. The ones, she remembered with a twinge, he apparently couldn't stand.

'Hi. How's it going?' he said cheerfully.

'Yeah, fine. I was just thinking of leaving actually.' She tried to sound casual.

'Oh.' He looked disappointed. Well, why didn't he ask her to stay, then? It was one of those moments when neither person wants to appear too keen, and in the end nothing is said at all. 'Well, are you all right to get back . . . I mean, on your own?'

'Yes, I think I can manage it,' she snapped.

The girl looked impatient and peeved at the amount of attention Marly was receiving.

'I've just got to say goodbye to the others. I'll see

you.' She managed a strained smile and walked away. Why was she so bothered by the whole thing? She knew how these things affected her and after various hearbreaks through her teenage years she'd sworn to herself never to allow that side of her to rear its head around men. She'd only just met him, she was in a new place, it was all getting out of hand. Walking up the stairs, giving herself a good talking to and feeling better for it, she reached the doors and Sean caught up with her.

'Um . . . Are you sure you'll be all right getting back. You look a bit wasted.'

'Oh, thanks for telling me. Look, I'm capable of catching a taxi, you know. We do have them at home.' She could hear her tone of voice and she didn't like it. It smacked of her mother. She was being wholly unreasonable. If anything was going to put him off it was this.

'OK . . . Look, shall I give you a ring or something?'

She wished she could stay now but she'd said too much and she didn't want him thinking it was just due to him.

'Yeah, OK, if you want to.' She cringed at the old line. Why would he ask otherwise?

'Right, then. Take care, love.' He squeezed her arm and went back downstairs.

She had to be content with that. She hadn't exactly made it easy for him, but then again, he was out with another girl.

She walked up to the cluster of cabbies hanging around Tottenham Court Road.

'Chalk Farm, please.'

'Been out dancing, have you?' He was impossibly cheery.

'Mmmm . . . Just around the corner.'

'So, are you at college or do you work, love?'

'I'm just about to start a job. I left college about a year and a half ago.' Normally she would have been on for a chat, but now she wished he'd just drive.

'Could I put the radio on?' she asked, hoping it might make the journey go quicker.

'Sorry, love, it's broken . . . So, what did you do at college?'

'Umm . . . European Lit.'

'Yeah? I used to have a couple of houses in Wolverhampton. Those bloody students, they pissed me about like anything. One girl, she used to sun-bathe topless in the garden. I said, I don't want none of that, my mother lives next door. My mum says to me, are you sleeping with this girl? I said, why, mum? She said, she's sitting naked in the garden. I told her to put some clothes on, eh, love? You know, politely like the first time. But she kept on. That's it, I said, and she said, I pay my rent, I can do what I like. I said, not in my house, you can't, and I threw her out. I had two beautiful nurses living in one. Salt of the earth, they were, but students . . . they're bad news. No offence, love. And then I'd have the parents on the phone com-plaining about the way I was treating their kids. The mothers were the worst. I'd say to them, he may be breaking your heart, lady, but he ain't fucking breaking mine. The problem is, see, we're all institutionalized from the day we're born. I'd love to be a teacher, not with bloody eighteen-year-olds but little kids, you know? I'd teach them a thing or two. My old headmaster told me I'd be digging ditches by the time I was twenty. He's in jail now for fraud. I picked him up for a fare a few years back. He said, how come you're driving round in a Merc? I hope you got it legal. Like, fucking cheek. O*h*, *no*, I says to him, you must be joking, I've been doing a bit of pimping, got a couple of nice birds working for me and of course the odd bit of dealing drugs . . . He said, all right, I didn't mean to insult you. I said, yeah, and I bet you didn't mean it when you said I'd end up digging fucking ditches, now get out of my cab . . . They told John Lennon he was tone deaf at school and stopped him taking music, the cunts. Jesus, I wish I'd met him, before he popped his clogs, the poor bastard, I got it all sorted . . . '

Her head was pounding as she finally climbed the stairs to the flat. She could hear the low thump of bass coming from Rover's, playing his favourite Osric Tentacles album. At this very moment he was probably forcing his way through half an ounce on his bong. She let herself into the darkened hall. The flat was still but there was music coming softly from Paul's room and she knocked quietly, but he didn't answer. She wasn't ready for bed and wondered if a joint or two would help her sleep.

She went downstairs and rang Rover's bell. He

answered straight away and looked delighted to have some company.

'All right there? You're up late. Bit of a night owl like me, are you? Do you want to come in?'

The flat was dimly lit with drab seventies furnishings. An old settee was covered with an ethnic throw, a low coffee table was crowded with fag butts, papers, an oil burner and a pack of Tarot cards. Rover was surrounded by a pile of cloth hats.

'What are they?' Marly asked.

'I'm, er . . . making, I mean fixing up, a load of these Peruvian shepherd hats to sell down the market at the weekend. Do you fancy a cup of tea?'

He went into the kitchen. Marly had a good look round. On the walls were posters of Bob Marley with a fat joint in his mouth and Jack Nicholson doing his 'Here's Johnny' bit from The Shining.

Amongst the junk on the mantelpiece was a family photo of Rover aged about ten with an amazing seventies haircut. His father was a long-haired, moustachioed beanpole and his mum the image of Cher in her 'I got you, babe' days.

She went off to use the loo while he brought in the tea.

'Sorry about all the stuff in there. It's a bit of a mess.'

She went in to find sheets of acid hanging up to dry. 'So how much of that do you make, then?'

'I've got these traveller mates who get me the base and I make it up and dip them and that, and we split the proceeds. Don't let on, though, will you? Not the sort of thing I'd like too many people getting wind of, if you catch my ball.' He laughed, then skinned up and passed it to her to light.

She breathed in the muggy smoke and felt her spine and neck relax. It was the best painkiller in the world, suffocating all the tenseness brought on by those tiny crystals running around her brain. The worries about Sean seemed to ease off too. The drawback, of course, was the beginnings of an urge to listen to and talk dross and enjoy it.

'Nice gear, this,' said Rover. 'Only problem is, I've been smoking more than I've been selling.'

'How much do you get through a day?' she asked, passing him the joint, perfectly rolled and slender as a straw.

'Depends. A lot.' He laughed. 'But you know what they say, "An eighth a day keeps reality away." So, what, you got a big family?' he asked politely.

'Yeah, I s'pose so. Not that big for Ireland. There's me, two older brothers, one in Australia, and three younger sisters. Two are twins, a bit weird – they never leave each other's sides.'

'Yeah, I can relate to that. I'm a Gemini,' said Rover mystically.

'Oh, right . . . Well . . . who's the person you're closest to?'

'Errr . . . Well, I suppose, like, I'm two people in one and, like, one can't do without the other.' He looked as confused as she felt.

'Where are your family, then?'

'Oh, um, well, my mum's down in Kent and I never talk to my dad.'

'Don't you get on?'

'No, I'm sure we'd get on fine, but he fucked off with my mum's best mate when I was fifteen.'

'Oh, I'm sorry. Your poor mum,' said Marly, concerned.

'What about me? I was shagging her too.'

'Oh, well . . . I'm sure it worked out for the best.' She tried not to laugh.

'Ahh . . . This is very pleasant. I like just sitting and chilling and, you know, talking to someone with a bit of sav. The world's just so full of bullshit sometimes. You know, it could be such a beautiful place . . .' Rover was off on one now. 'But it's all just so . . . fucked. Do you know what I mean?'

'Ummm? . . . Oh, yeah . . . sure.' Marly's eyes were beginning to feel heavy.

'It's like, there's a lot of anger around . . . and a lot of pain, and it's really hard to find a sort of – what's the word? – Europa, where everyone can just be happy.'

'Utopia,' corrected Marly.

'Eh? Oh, yeah, Utopia . . . Anyway, I used to have this real problem with, like, who I was . . . and where I was . . . and why I was or wasn't there . . .' Marly was fighting her eyelids now. 'And I knew I had to sort my head out, so I just took off with a few close mates, a drum and my Psychic Warriors of Gaia album and went off to Surrey for the weekend.'

'And what did you do?'

'Well, we got right into our percussion and cried and hugged a little and got in touch with our anger and pain . . . and our massive drug habits, and eventually got to the place.'

'Where's that? I don't know Surrey.'

'No . . . It's not on no map,' said Rover cryptically. 'It's, like, the land of contentment.'

'That's, er . . . I mean, I'm really pleased for you. Oh . . .' She yawned widely. 'It's late. I'd better get off to bed. Thanks for the smoke.'

'Yeah. Must do it again soon.' He winked and gave her a bit of a once-over as she climbed the stairs.

Back in her room she lay down on the mattress and shut her eyes. Sleep still evaded her and she tried to ignore the random images that were flooding her mind. The music from Paul's room came through the wall and made her body move gently in time against her will.

Eight

Work quickly became a bind for Marly. She realized how many job titles there were for dogsbody in the world of media: production assistant, runner, assistant to the producer, personal assistant, arse wiper. Different girls appeared in the office each day: Becky, Vicky, Jakki, Sammi, Tammy, all chattering and nattering about holistic medicine, massage, their director boyfriend's fantastic new scripts, the fabulous restaurant they'd gone to last night, where they'd bumped into Nicole and Tom – well, they were on the next table anyway – and lastly what they were going to have for lunch today. It was gonna have to be ciabatta, artichoke and sun-dried, drizzled with a little walnut oil – again.

Still, Marly did like Nicky, who, as Nick had promised, treated her well. The boredom did get to her, though, and she resorted to making endless phone calls when Nicky was out. She wished she'd taken Sean's number. He probably wouldn't call her after her bratty strop the other night.

She tried Kate's extension, but she was out, so she asked to be put back to reception, where Dani picked up the phone and gabbled on about how she'd almost swung it with Oliver, but 'that bitch of a model, who incidentally should be retiring soon, seeing as she's hitting the big 3-0', was hanging around him all night. I do think he definitely likes me, though.'

Marly didn't like to say he couldn't even remember Dani's name when Marly had asked him if he'd seen her lately. He'd then promptly tried to stick his tongue down Lee's throat in the club on Tuesday night after Marly had gone home.

Dani was OK. From a rich Jewish north London family, she had a lot of the proverbial chutzpah. She was great fun and even though she was a little neurotic about herself and constantly worried about turning into her mother, she never stayed down for long. Marly liked her sparkle and enthusiasm, even if the life she led was a bit of a sham sometimes. Nothing mattered if you were young. You were allowed to make mistakes and act like a fool. Marly knew she did her fair share.

Tonight, said Dani, they were going to a Shove It party at a 'secret location' in west London, which happened to be a dodgy old disused film studio. She asked if Marly wanted to come.

'Frankie FeelUp and Mickey Tinsel are playing. Oliver says they're really good. He's the one who told me about it. I hope he turns up. I've bought this beautiful two-piece from Lounge Lizard – £90, but it's worth it.'

H's flu was easing off by the weekend and he took it upon himself to arrange another meeting on BB's behalf at Simone's flat on Friday night.

'Why do they have to come here, H.' she moaned from the kitchen. 'I was gonna cook you spaghetti bolognese tonight and I got that *Speed* out on video – you know, with Keanu Reeves.'

'Oh, yeah. I wonder why you got that one.' He scowled jealously. 'Anyway, the boys are coming over. We've got a few things to sort out. BB's bringing his gear round to try and finish that Dutch track. I though we could set it up in your bedroom with your computer, plus we might be stepping out later on.'

'Stepping out where?'

'Just *out*!'

'Well, what about the film?'

'You can watch it round Tina's, can't you?'

He went off to dig out some extension leads and left Simone standing there, tearful, with the video in one hand and a jar of Ragù in the other.

The boys arrived around nine. BB was nervous and had spent a good few hours beforehand sizing up the situation and deciding what to say. He'd recovered from his 'temporary insanity' and wanted to propose another plan of action for the following night. This time nothing was going to stop him, especially not his own lack of self-control.

'Where's the *missus*, H?' he sneered, his old contemptuous self back in action, he was relieved to find.

'Round her mate's . . . I had to promise her a trip up the Harvester on Sunday for chicken in a basket. I thought she was never going to leave.'

'She got any skins lying around?' asked Col, getting his priorities right.

'In her bedroom, I think, next to the, er, them things – you know, er . . . Tampax.'

'Urgh,' said Col. 'Go on, Baz, you get them.'

BB's ideas were slow in coming. Virgil wanted to use a high-frequency animal call as a sample in the track. The others weren't too sure.

'It sounds like my fucking old dear having a go when I leave my shit on the kitchen table,' said Baz. '"I told you not to smoke that rubbish in my house. Wait till I tell your dad. He'll have you out. I've just about had enough,"' he imitated in a high-pitched nag.

Wiz lapsed into his hyena cackle.

'Well, I like it,' said Virgil sulkily.

The hours passed slowly and they were getting nowhere. H was bored so he took half a trip on the sly and kept forgetting to save various parts they'd programmed into the computer. Baz and Col eked out their dope stingily, to make sure it lasted the night, while both separately, secretly keeping a joint or two's worth back from one another for the next morning. Wiz and his cousin, down from Scotland, talked most of the time about their favourite conspiracy theories, ranging from Neil Armstrong's purported alien sightings on the moon to the secret 'club' you had to be in if you wanted a job on children's TV: 'I'm telling you, mate,' said Wiz, 'they all bat for the other team.'

BB felt his whole crusade was beginning to crumble around his ears. The crazy events of the past few nights must be put behind him, even if it meant going back to square one.

'I think we need a little break. How about we take a meander up west and get a little action? You got your wheels sorted yet, Baz?'

The van was all-important in the game. They'd all seen *Silence of the Lambs* and it added the necessary chill factor to their clubber-kidnap fantasy. As BB said while they all climbed in, 'No van, no plan.'

The pulse of the room flooded Marly's body. She felt as if her heart was expanding with each beat and her brain tingled with the familiar snowstorm of drugs swirling around inside her. Her skull felt tight and she took a deep breath and held on to the bar to steady herself. She'd be fine in a minute, she told herself, as she fought off a massive wave of paranoia about brain haemorrhages. Then the music caught her off guard and brought her back to a more conscious state. Sometimes it worked like that and sometimes it did the reverse. The music could take control, making the crowd feel like it was the most powerful thing on earth. The cult of uniting under a banner of common pleasure was an easy and natural thing.

The music rippled on and on. Marly's brain was on a roller-coaster of highs and lows. She felt the only thing that ranked above it must be the DJ's euphoria watching the whole thing. Music like that was appealing because it was unhindered by words that meant too much. Someone else's thoughts put up boundaries to understanding.

That first night she sat up with Paul, he'd said he didn't care: 'Who gives a fuck what U2 or Prince have to say? The best songs are silly ones, Madness or Motown, or songs written when you're out of your head, like Bowie or Jimi Hendrix, who wrote what came out of the drugs. And that all depends on what drugs you stick inside you. You can tell the ones written on cocaine. All over the shop, like disco. That's hokey-cokey – over-the-top strings and reach-for-the-skies vocals. But it was all right because it was for the first time. House did it for me for a while. Now it's all gone commercial and the whole thing is cynical as fuck. They know people will come up on any old tune, so they're putting out conveyor-belt music with keys that hit the right spots, all strategically placed so you feel uplifted. The drugs are shit now too. You don't know what you're getting in your Es, but they're better than nothing at the end of the day . . . and the government's saying there's a problem with young people's drug taking. There's a problem all right . . . the drugs aren't working.'

She'd though about what he'd said. Paul's manner of speech was infectious. Within ten days she'd even found herself swearing more than ever. The act of swearing was not a revolt any more. It was as common in the streets as litter. Not that she cared, she'd just noticed herself: 'I'm fucked' meaning she was tired, drugged up, in trouble; 'fucking about' was doing anything you wanted; girls said 'cunt' to mean idiot and no one batted an eye. You got more notice if you spoke a sentence without a profanity. People would look at you 'funny' and say you were a bit straight, up-tight, old-fashioned.

Marly remembered the first swear words she'd ever heard and understood had been in a song. She was eight and listening to a John Lennon single – 'Working Class Hero'. She'd played it three times to make sure she'd heard right: she didn't understand what it all meant exactly but it made her feel grown-up and part of the adult world she'd longed to join, watching her older brothers buying punk and then ska records, going to Specials gigs and she at home secretly listening to those records, gazing at the front covers, falling in love with the big older boys in the photos with their Crombies, crew cuts and big, doleful eyes. When it came to Marly's turn, she found herself disappointed with the choice of music idols on offer. She suffered through poncy, lipsticked and powdered asexual types pouting and posturing to their tinny, harsh and loveless records with a false grace that matched the synthesized chords they put in their songs. She came to realize that was how music grew. It all added up. Each progression was an innovation because it brought some kind of reaction.

Tonight Nick was around in the club somewhere. He'd called earlier as they were getting ready to go out. She'd decided to strike Sean off her list of hopes for the future. He was obviously a bit of a flake, and she might well have been simply a little diversion for the weekend.

Nick's friend Sol, a smooth clapper loader, came up and shook her by the arm, flashing a wide, slick smile. Somehow she knew he was going to say it: 'Cheer up. It might never happen . . . Do you want a drink?'

She dug up a smile. 'Yes please. I'll have a beer.'

As with Nick, he still seemed to regard nightclubs as pulling grounds. It was probably due to their age. In Kate's words, they were 'a bit seventies'.

Kate was getting the brunt of Nick's charm in the corner, while Lee and a girlfriend from work were dancing. Lee looked like a fucked-up Bond girl, all slinky-kitten charm tempered with an E-induced weariness. She was looking extra-glamourous; as she said on the way to the club, everything had gone right tonight. Marly couldn't help noticing how thin she was. She considered saying something to her later, perhaps a hint about an article in V*ogue* on healthy eating, but then thought better of it – Lee was a big girl.

Sol wouldn't piss off, so she suggested they join the others. An old anthem, 'I Believe', came on and the dance floor shifted moods. The monotony of the track tired her out quickly. The fake stars twinkled on the ceiling above the dance floor. She kept looking up, thinking she was seeing them for real through a skylight. She felt like she was drowning in a sea of glitter. The hypnosis wasn't working tonight and she suddenly felt like she needed some air. She stumbled outside to the small garden, greenly lit and laced with plastic vines, and sat on a plant pot. She stared straight ahead, trying to focus her thoughts. Up in the sky were strange lights that seemed to zigzag and stop and start. If she could have trusted her judgement she would have got excited at the prospect of UFOs. She felt a hand on her leg. It was Sol.

'So, you're a bit of a stargazer. Just like me.'

Marly's head was reeling. She needed a joint to calm her nerves. Sol obliged, taking pride in his origami technique. They smoked it and she hung her head, unable to cope with the surroundings for a moment. He took it as a cue to start rubbing her neck 'sensuously'. She didn't have the strength or the drive to tell him to stop and after a while it was actually quite nice. He was a touch *too* good-looking for her tastes, too slick. He bent his head round and mumbled something incoherently. She looked up and in a flash he was kissing her. For some reason, she couldn't push him off – they were trapped in the record that was playing. Only after a good two minutes did she break with a mixture of surprise and amusement. She wondered if her lipstick was all over her face and then remembered she wasn't wearing any. She looked around her. Just across from her, standing alone under a white arch was Sean.

'I'm such a slag,' she wailed to Lee in the loos an hour later. 'Why do you have to lose all your taste on drugs? Any old dodgy arsehole becomes the most thrilling man on earth . . . well, for about ten minutes anyway.'

'Oh, don't be so stupid. Forget it. He will. If Sean couldn't be arsed to phone you, then he's not worth bothering about. You shouldn't be wanting to get involved. You've only just got here, for fuck's sake. Now shut up and have a line. Go on, it's not mine. Sol told me to help myself.' Lee giggled.

'Sol's, is it? Right, get chopping.'

The boys stopped at the all-night garage to stock up on fags, papers and Quavers for Colin. Baz went in with him.

'Have you said anything to any of the others yet?' he asked furtively.

'About what?'

'About, you know . . . the other night. When we heard that . . . stuff coming from . . . you-know-who's room,' he murmured out of the corner of his mouth.

'No . . . Have you?'

'No way. I still don't believe it. I mean, I believe I heard it and that, but there's got to be a reason. Maybe he was, like, exploring the psyche of the enemy. He doesn't do things by half, BB.'

'Yeah . . . yeah, that's it.'

They drove down the Harrow Road and made their way towards the centre. BB wanted to do something spontaneous tonight, to strike out of the dark, fast and furious. He thought of going back to Pinacoladarada as a kind of revenge for what had taken place the week before, for hoodwinking him, for turning him into a puppet and pulling the strings. They stopped at a red light.

'I feel lucky tonight. What say we try our hand at a little light abduction?'

A collective cheer went up in the back of the van.

'Where to, Chief?' said Wiz, getting carried away. He'd be singing the 'Self-preservation Society' song next.

'Hold it. Stop the van. I want to get out,' cried H all of a sudden. He'd spotted the two clubbers from his handbag night out. They parked and he ran across the road. Kyle and Shireen had trouble recognizing him. They looked at his dowdy grey sweatshirt and green jeans in disbelief.

'All right there? Where you off to tonight, then?'

'So, what's the score? Where's the fucking "place to be" tonight, H?' asked BB as H got back in the van.

'They're going to some big do in west London. I've

got the address. It's one of them ticket-only jobs, with loads of novelty rooms and big-name DJs.'

'Hmm . . . Sounds like the jackpot. Let's take a gamble.'

Marly couldn't see him anywhere. She went up the spiral staircase and peered over the crowd, but to no avail. She did, however, spot Sol making his way across the room towards her and she ran into the chill-out room to escape. She sat down on a big, clear plastic blow-up chair and listened to Mickey Tinsel's set. The dance floor was virtually empty, bar one or two happy souls, lost in space, looking like they would have danced to the sound of fire alarms if someone set them off, one grinning at the ceiling, the other, eyes shut, dancing like a retarded snake. She stared at his wild undulations, her own mind cloudy with dope and E. His arms left a trail of light as he moved them around his head. She couldn't watch any more, lowering her eyes to put out her cigarette. Two pairs of legs appeared. She looked up with difficulty. It was Kate and Sean.

Great, was her first thought, he's probably after her now. Kate, however, said she'd get some drinks and smiled encouragingly at her. He sat down in the seat opposite.

'Having a good time?' he asked without a trace of irony.

'Um, yeah, well, I think so.' She wanted to blurt the whole thing out, how she wished she'd never met that bloke, but she wasn't sure he even cared or wanted to know. His eyes were huge and soft, like polished minerals. Why did he make her go weak whenever he looked at her?

Kate set down two bottles of water and sipped her Coke standing up.

'Oh, shit. I've just remembered Lee's got my gear. I'll be back in a sec.' She departed tactfully.

'What have you been up to, then?' she asked, looking at the crowd opposite, who were lying all over one another. She wondered if they'd just met.

'I've been in the studio for the last two days, overseeing a session with this new girl singer. I'm trying to put her with these two blokes who do trip hop and ambient stuff. She's got a top voice, but it was the first time they met.'

'And?'

'Yeah, it turned out fine. In fact, I think one of the blokes ended up going out with her tonight. Bad move, but what can you do?'

She laughed. If only he'd turned up a bit earlier, they'd be sitting here without reason not to go for it, she thought with regret.

'I'm pretty tired.' He looked at his watch. 'It's fucking five o'clock. I promised myself I'd get an early one tonight. I've got to go to Manchester tomorrow.'

'You mean today.'

'Yeah . . . Do you want me to wait till Kate gets back?'

'No, no . . . I'm fine here.'

'Right, then.' He bent down and kissed her cheek,

brushing her hair with his hand. She shivered at his touch and looked up. 'See you soon,' he said with a grin and was gone.

She sat alone in the chair. The pitch of the music had turned nasty somehow and the faces in the room looked strange and distorted.

'Who's got my Bounty?' asked Col angrily.

A chorus of nos resounded from all parties.

'Look, it was in that bag from the garage. Someone's got it,' he accused.

'Um, Col, mate. I think you're . . . Get up from your seat a sec, will you?' offered Baz. There it was flattened and gooey, stuck to his rear.

'Colin! Couldn't you have waited?' Wiz 'joked' in hysterics.

They sat patiently in the van, listening to Baz's new car stereo, playing techno tapes that didn't come across too well on a £10 Realistic flat-face model.

Virg and Ronnie, Wiz's cousin, slept for a while. No one had any cash to buy stimulants to keep them awake, apart from Wiz, who lived for his speed. At about half-five, the crowds started trickling out. BB sat up, drawing his wits about him.

'Looks like this is it. Our time has come,' he said prophetically.

The van doors opened and they crept out of the shadows, armed with a couple of sacks from Baz's dad's fruit stall and a roll of extra-strength gaffer tape. They spotted a couple of lads walking uncertainly down the steps, both wearing checked open shirts with sunglasses perched on top of their heads.

'Fucking shades at this time of night, and in the middle of autumn,' BB whispered with venom.

'We'll soon sort *them* out.'

Marly and the girls managed to find a call box and rang a cab, after thankfully losing Sol. She imagined he'd probably moved on to someone else by now. Still in a daze over Sean, she couldn't get his face out of her mind.

'Here we go,' said Lee as the cab pulled up.

Back at Chalk Farm, they sat smoking and watching kids' TV, waiting for sleep to calm them. Marly took a bath to while away an hour. She was drying her hair as she heard Paul come in. He looked fresh-faced and exhilarated as she went into the living room.

'That's it. It's all happening,' he crowed.

'Eh?' said Lee.

'I've been down Brixton at the new studio all night. I moved all my gear in in Adam's van. Martin, that bloke I was telling you about, he's paid up the bill for the next four months. Me, Dave and Ad have been in there all night working.'

'Yeah, right, working.' laughed Lee.

She went to bed and fell asleep straight away. Tonight her mind insisted on assessing everything that had happened. She was in a large blue room with a deep pool in the middle. Someone was trying to push her in, but her feet were chained with heavy manacles to a horrible ancient-looking statue. Her hair was trailing in the water and she submerged her face and looked into the depths. An enormous fish slowly circled the bottom. It started to rise towards her, it's eyes looking at her intently. The dream changed then and she was in a huge house looking for someone she knew. Blank faces passed her by and smiled, but she didn't stop. She couldn't see anyone that meant anything to her. She climbed out of a window and saw a car waiting on the street. She called but the car pulled away. It was Sean, surrounded by faceless people. Someone tapped her on the shoulder. She turned around and it was Paul, who pulled her off out of the house and into a vast open space. They ran on and on, heading for the wild blue yonder . . . She woke up to the sound of drilling on the road outside.

Nine

'**W**hat do you want with us?' said the first boy, terror rising in his muffled voice. The two sat bolt upright on steel-backed chairs in Col's dad's lock-up, their heads covered with the sacking and their hands tightly bound with tape.

'Where are my fucking shades?' said the other bravely. 'My fucking Cutler and Gross. They cost me seventy-five quid. If they're broken I'll –'

'You'll what?' said BB as he dropped them on the floor and slowly ground them to a mangled ball of plastic. The boy cried out at the loud crunch.

'Look, what the hell's going on here? I've got money if you –'

'Oh, yeah. How much have –' began H.

He was silenced with a look from BB. 'We want to educate you,' he said in his best Kray-twin growl.

'What do you mean?'

His friend started to cry.

BB raised a hand, signalling Virg to start the music. Malevolent, vile sounds came blaring out of the speakers as black as the night, pounding through the cold and hollow room. The two captives sat, enduring their worst nightmare, while the AHL, the fruits of their labour rewarded at last, stood around laughing long and loud and danced around the pair like savages. The screams rang out into the morning, unheard through the music and the thick walls.

'YOU DO LIKE ITT . . . GO ON, SAY ITT . . . By the time we've finished with you, you won't even know your own names.'

'What are their names?' whispered Wiz.

'SHUT UP,' snarled BB, riding on a wave of megalomania. 'DANCE, YOU BASTARDS, DANCE.'

The unhappy pair rose shakily to their feet, prodded by Wiz with his Luke SkyWalker plastic light-sabre. They began to shuffle their feet slowly, keeping in time as best they could with the jerky, arhythmic drone.

'Chief, let us do a Chinese burn, go on . . . please,' simpered Wiz in twisted delight.

BB was tempted, but held on to reason by fragile reins.

It was a long morning. Virgil went out for supplies. The boys begged for some Purdy's Elixir, but their pleas fell on deaf ears.

'But we're dying of thirst,' they whimpered.

'No,' replied Virgil. 'Those bods in Ethiopia were dying of thirst . . . Anyway that's what you get for sweating all night at some poncy fucking 18–30s club,' he laughed. A flood of guilt washed over BB. It soon passed.

The torture continued. Virgil recited a catalogue of the weirdest techno tunes he could think of, serial numbers and all, over the top of the music. At midday, the two lads cracked. They repeated the names of all the top techno clubs, DJs, tunes and even a short history of the genre. Their clothes lay in tatters at their feet, replaced by grim black T-shirts embossed with the most satanic computer-generated designs, murky coloured baggy cords and brown, heavy, scuffed Timberlands.

'We love techno. It is our life. Never again shall we succumb to the temptations of handbag,' they repeatedly moaned after Wiz.

At about two, the van screeched to a halt in the middle of Pinner High Street. The sacks were removed from their heads and the two boys were thrown on to a grassy verge.

'AND MAKE SURE YOU TELL YOUR FRIENDS, YOU STUPID FUCKS!'

The van zoomed off into the distance before they came to their considerably disturbed senses.

*

Sean called Marly on Sunday afternoon, much to her amazement. He'd just got back from Manchester and asked if she fancied coming out for a drink later. As much as she wanted to appear ice cool, she agreed straight away. Lee heard this and gave her a good talking-to.

'You're fucking hopeless. You should have said maybe and *then* turned up unexpectedly.'

'Oh, who cares? If he's that transparent, I don't want to know.'

'Thanks very much!' Lee went off in a strop.

She went through the usual trauma of deciding what to wear.

'Well, he'll probably take you out somewhere later. So wear your new Agnes B skirt and that little pink jumper. You can borrow my Patrick Coxes, and then bring a top and some heels with you,' advised Kate. 'Are you going to stay over there?'

'Oh . . . I don't know.'

'Didn't you . . . that first night? I thought you . . .'

'No, no. We just sat around talking and that.'

'What a pair,' sighed Lee as she came back into the kitchen.

Marly got to Sean's about eight. He was just about to order a Thai takeaway.

'Have you eaten?'

She shook her head.

They drank a bottle of Chardonnay with the food,

then headed down the pub.

'There's a night on at the Square. My mate's DJing and I said I'd try and pop down. Do you want to go?'

'Yeah . . . What kind of music?'

'Progressive house, weird stuff his mates have done, or tracks he gets sent over from the States.'

'Did you ever DJ?'

'Years ago, before you had to be a showbiz person- ality to get on and put up with groupies.' He laughed.

They stopped off at the flat to phone a cab and Sean brought out some coke.

'Do you want a line?'

'Umm . . . Yeah, all right.' She was a bit taken aback, surprised that he always seemed to have drugs on the go, or maybe this was a special occasion, she hoped.

The cab took them down to Farringdon and they walked straight in past the bouncer, who smiled at Sean and gave him a regular's greeting.

Sunday night was a little more subdued. The crowd seemed more serious and uniform. Saturdays were always a mixed bag, with a few odd-bod tourists and out-of-town drinkers who came in for a 'night out on the tiles', uninterested in the musical content or in fol- lowing a particular scene. This bunch at the Square knew what they'd come for and expected it to be top- notch. Sean asked her to get some drinks while he sorted something out. The bar staff clocked she was with him and smiled broadly. Marly reasoned he must be a regular face or even a vague celebrity to get that kind of reaction. He came back and took a sip of his beer, bit a small white pill in two and popped one half into her mouth. She was annoyed he hadn't asked her but felt stupid protesting now.

They danced for a bit when Sean's mate came on. The music was eclectic, a multi-faceted wave, with all kinds of styles and sounds, totally different to the stuff she'd heard the other night. More percussion and bass and stranger moods. The crowd loved it.

Mark, the DJ, came and sat with them after his set. A few trainspotters were hanging around their table, wanting to come and congratulate him but resisting for coolness's sake. Marly found this all very strange, a kind of hero-worship. She remembered what Sean had said about the status of DJs. All they did was play records, other people's at that, and although she credited their knack for putting the right ones together, surely rock and roll was the only scene you were supposed to get *that* excited about.

A couple of girls joined them, die-hard DJ groupies, serious-faced, simple make-up and hair, wearing obscure record label T-shirts and bondage trousers. Both were beautiful, but their beauty was marred by a permanent worried scowl, either from the drugs or the pressure of maintaining a steady flow of 'chill'. It struck Marly that girls like these, however bright or special in their own right, would always be suffocated by the pecking order of this bloky world. Girls had their place and they'd better not forget it. She remembered a story she'd read about a rock chick, who was having a bad time on smack. She went to her boyfriend's concert, feeling down and probably not looking her best. The singer boyfriend happened to spot another temptress backstage, fresh and on top form, and dumped his girl for her, kicking her when she was down. Girls, it seemed, were expendable. When they didn't cut it any more, they were out.

Her pill was doing its thing now, headier than ever before, probably due to the drink. She went off to dance and was joined shortly after by the other girls, who cracked her a rare smile. She glanced over and saw Sean and Mark looking at her and talking. She couldn't help worrying if she looked all right. These places inspired that kind of feeling. She remembered the old-style raves she used to go to in the country with Kate, before the Criminal Justice Bill – how everyone looked the same, desexed and totally relaxed. This body-conscious Hollywood syndrome had replaced all that, and although it was fun to dress up, it was exhausting.

When they sat back down, Mark was talking about his recent holiday in Portugal.

'Yeah, man, Ibiza's had it. It's turned into a fucking holiday camp. You go on holiday to escape from England and over there you're always running into people from home. Last summer I just had enough. We rented a villa and it got invaded by a load of spongers and wideboys. I want a place which is foreign but up with the music and that. I'm telling you, you should take a little trip to Lisbon. The South of France is all right too, bit pricey but you get your space and its fucking beautiful to look at. They're putting on some wicked outdoor parties at the moment. And, present company excepted and that –' he smiled at Marly – 'but the women are the fittest . . .'

Sean's flat was full of music memorabilia – kitsch gifts from friends, freebies he'd picked up on jobs – all telling of the kind of life he'd led. His past was in everything: the obligatory electric and acoustic guitars stood dusty in the corner, symbols of his youth when he was trying his luck in bands; a vast record and CD collection covered the walls, Beastie Boys, the Beat, the B52s to the Sex Pistols, the Slits and Supergrass. She noticed a photo of a little boy on the mantelpiece, standing on a beach holding a woman's hand. She didn't ask but he was undoubtedly related to Sean, the same eyebrows and the same smile.

Mark and his girlfriend arrived in her two-seater. They knocked on the window and Marly opened the door while Sean went into the shower. She felt uneasy acting the hostess in a place where she didn't know her role yet. When she looked back, she and Sean had hardly spoken, except for superficial babble about places to go, favourite music, gossip. But this was the way you grew to know someone. Little by little those surface layers came away with each hour. Each minor conversation meant something as it probed deeper through the shell of a public face and shed another protective skin. Finally, when you ran out of trivial air, you got the real thing. The real thing with Sean, however, was indistinct and shadowed. He seemed to have slow-waltzed through life, taking things as they came. He reminded her of the boy at school that everyone looked up to for his effortless cool and charm. She sat there with Tanya, chatting about London life, Tanya spilling the beans on the sordid sex set-ups of a few top names in clubland.

'They've been living together for years as husband and husband and there's all those girls who follow them around, hoping to cop off . . . If only they knew.'

And all the while Marly was distracted in her drifting haze, wanting to be alone with him. Sean came into the room and opened a small bag of pills. God, they were always around, so tempting in their promise of a better night. She knew that certain things in life had a spark of their own, but that chance of improving them . . . She took the pill in his hand, thinking she didn't want to miss out. Tonight could be a memory she'd always cherish, among others.

Mark and Tanya left around three. It was a night of fumbling for Marly and Sean. They lay in bed and held each other, listening to old Studio One dub. The low, heavy sounds were arousing in their heady combination of delayed throbbing bass and drums, but Sean never once reached the stage where he was even slightly out of control. He lay stroking her hair and kissing her but was strangely distant. At first she worried it was her, that she was lacking in some way, and was embarrassed to push him onwards. The confusion of being with him like this without the natural moves made her tense. She tried to sleep but her chemical alertness struggled against the impulse. Gradually the motion of the music took over, sending her mind into a slow spin. She relaxed and tried to accept him as he was, pleasant, gentle and still. He finally slept and she quietly got up, unable to drift off with him. She sat by the window and watched the sun come up, wishing she knew him better.

Ten

Time passes in the city like the river at its heart. From a distance rolling on languorously, gently persuading its waves and ripples along. Up close it flows fast and swirls dangerously, greedy and urgent, controlling all that lies in its bounds. Before Marly knew it, it was the beginning of October. She went home for a few days to see her brother get married to an American girl. The prospect of playing hostess to a bevy of 'enthusiastic' tourists in her house was an unwelcome one. She found, however, that it took the focus of attention off her, and she was able to merge in without the usual barrage of questions about her new life. Her mother's only comment had been how thin and pale she looked.

'I've been working really hard, that's all,' was Marly's reassuring reply.

Her friend Fran came round to see her. They hugged and over-exaggerated about how the other had changed and sat down to gossip. Marly had almost forgotten how different the priorities of conversation were in Ireland. Gossip was an art form and judgements were passed easily and quickly on others, especially strangers. Fran talked about a new family in the village who'd 'just bought the Cassidys' house . . . and it's just not the same. I suppose it never will be, now Tom Cassidy's gone –'

'What do you mean . . . gone?' Marly put her cup down slowly.

'Didn't your mum . . .' Fran paused for an awful moment. 'Tom died. He was killed about a month ago. Your mum probably didn't want to . . . I mean, I know how you used to have a thing about him and –'

'How? . . . What happened?' Marly lit a cigarette with pale, trembling hands. She felt sick to the stomach.

'Well, you know he went up to Dublin last year and had that job, and everyone said he was earning good money and got his life in order? Well, it all turned out to be a bit of a sham. My brother went up to see him in the summer. Apparently he'd lost the job, he was doing drugs all the time and living with some weird girl who kept cutting herself up or something. Anyway, he came back home with no money and in a really bad way about a week after you left. He was in the pub all the time or just sitting around the place. I saw him once or twice, but it was like he wasn't there anymore. I mean, you remember what he was like at school . . .'

According to the local Garda, Tom had gone out one evening for a stroll, so he told his mother. They found him the next morning near the tracks. The train driver didn't even know he'd hit anyone till he got back to the station.

'Why? . . . Why did he do it?' But she believed she knew. She couldn't cry. She'd forgotten about Tom for a long time, but he'd always been the blue boy of her childhood, the figure she dreamed would be her future. He'd been as famous in their little town as Georgie Best or any pop star. He was the one every boy looked up to then and every girl wanted to look at her. The first to smoke, to get a Grade I haircut, to start a band. He was always up with the trends of the Big Smoke. He laughed like a maniac and had mood swings as deep and treacherous as the neighbouring sea. Bored with the monotony of life at home, he would go on lost weekends to Dublin and at fourteen even caught the boat train to London to see his favourite band. The town would huddle and gossip together in fear and ignorance at his waywardness and spirit of adventure.

Marly sat frozen to the spot, the image of his face filling her head. She remembered his eyes most of all, rare and powerful, darkest blue, which used to make her think of wet skies and winter dusk whenever he looked at her. She shivered.

'My brother reckons the drugs got to him,' Fran continued.

Marly thought different. He had gone in search of something bright, something shining on a distant hill. His home had never given him what he wanted, so he looked for it elsewhere, in the company of strangers, but found only discontent.

'I don't think he ever would have been happy, Marly. He wanted too much out of life.'

'Don't say that.' The tears welled up in her eyes, of anger as much as sorrow. 'He would have found something, I know he would . . . What a fucking waste.'

'And the blinding one-nighter, Crimes of Fashion, taking place, AS ALWAYS down at Bentleys every Saturday. BRRRinging you the very BEST Chicago DJs for another night of madness you WON'T FORGET. Stylish decor, comfortable chill-out rooms and high-tech vibrating dance floor making for a unique blend of mind-blowing mixes and a delicious cocktail of BEATS, BAD BEHAVIOUR AND BEAUTIFUL PEOPLE . . . BE THERE, BENTLEYS, EVERY SATURDAY . . .'

The maniacal, over-excited voice spewed out its stream of promo babble in between toon after toon of energy-packed tinny din played by the serious toned 'jock' who told London 'how it is'. Lee liked dedication time the best. She normally switched on of a night as they cooked dinner.

'Just like to say thanks for a wicked night last Saturday to all my mates down at the Sawmill. Special thanks to Dale in the leather trousers who made my night. Love to see you again sometime . . .'

'Sammi, Zoe and Fi, those bionic babes of Norwood, want to say their thank-yous to all their "wild bunch" down at the Underground. keep those butts moving and grooving and let's get together and have it on the dance floor again soon.'

'Big shout going out to all you Naughty but Nice regulars. Keep your mind free and your body in motion. Thanks for all the great nights we've had together. Till our next mental meeting . . . in Hell.'

'Fucking *sad*.' said Lee, laughing her husky rasp.

'I don't know,' said Kate kindly. 'I mean, if one of you lot did that, I'd think it was a laugh.'

'If one of our lot did it they wouldn't fucking be one of our lot any more, I can tell you.'

'Well, of course, we can't all be as ice cool as you, you "hip" thing, you.' Kate mussed Lee's hair up as she sat down next to her to eat, sending her into a mini-rage.

They went into the lounge after dinner and sat with Paul, who was having a rare night in. He was taking a break from the studio as Martin, his 'backer', was using it for someone else that week.

'Who's that, then?' asked Lee, sniffing around for a chance of a celebrity meeting.

'I don't know. Martin was a bit sketchy with the details. One of his American mates probably. He said there might be a chance of us working together, for cash, so I don't want to blow it by being pushy.'

'You're not pushy enough mate. You've got to go after what you want. What's he like anyway?'

'Martin? He's all right – bit quiet and that, but he's got some good ideas. He was saying how he reckons we should set up our own label, start putting our own stuff out. It wouldn't cost that much to get a thousand or so slapped up.'

Lee was trying to arrange her twenty-third birthday, which fell at the end of October, and she wanted to make it a night (or two) she'd never remember. The plan was to go to a Restoration weekender in a big house in the country, and it was being organized by a friend of Philippe's called Pansy, a hard-nosed Mancunian ex-dancer with a brilliant imagination and a flair for putting together the most dazzling nights in the country. Tickets were pricey, £20 from select joints around town, but Kate was pulling a few strings at her mag to get some freebies. Lee's brother was going to drive down from Colchester to pick them up and Kerry and Lisa were taking the Monday off in preparation for the inevitable 'drugover' they planned to have. Marly had even asked Sean a week beforehand so he'd keep it clear, but his response had been typically vague: 'See what happens, eh? I could be working.' He knew Pansy from home, years back, and wasn't one to get excited about her extravaganzas, which he found a little too camp for his liking.

Philippe and his once-upon-a-time partner, now flatmate, Gervase were round at the Chalk Farm flat too, deciding on costumes, one for each day of the weekend.

'I still say let's go for the Barbra Streisand look in *Hello Dolly* – you know, feathers . . . sequins . . . corsets, the works.'

Lee had been concerned with the problem of finding the money for the dress she'd spotted and just *had* to have for the occasion. In true fairy-tale fashion they had each chipped in £20 and left it on her bed when she'd come in from a hard day's work a week earlier. Her pleasure knew no bounds.

'Oh, you fucking lovely bastards,' she cried and laughed as she stripped off and slipped it on.

The venue was on the Wales/England border and Damien, Lee's big brother, picked them up in London in his Discovery on the Friday evening. He and his girlfriend were only staying at the party for the night session as she was seven months pregnant and, in her own words, 'having to slow things down a bit these days'.

Ragley Hall stood out on an incline above the M4. They could see a stream of cars going slowly up the drive as they approached. The girls were doing lines in the back, singing along to a remix of 'I Feel Love', while Paul and Damien shared a joint in the front. Marly sat next to Lucy discussing names for the baby.

'Damien says he wants something straight and normal. He reckons his own name's haunted him all his life, you know, everyone calling him 'Spawn of Satan' at school and that.'

'Well if it's a boy you could always call it Jesus, sort of balance things out,' offered Marly.

'Oh yeah, fucking nice life he'd have,' Damien piped up from the front. 'Twelve creepy blokes in dresses hanging around all the time, a chippie for a dad, no sex and dead at thirty . . . Nice.'

Philippe was meeting them there. Sean had said he'd give Marly a call via the reception if he was coming. He had to sit in on a session, he said, until ten or eleven, but he'd try and get a lift with Oliver's crowd. Philippe had booked a big room to use as a base, where they could crash out, get changed, have a shower or 'entertain gentleman callers', as Lee said hopefully.

Marly hadn't seen Sean in over a week and was feeling a bit despairing and in the dark about things. He'd been very sweet about her bad news from Ireland, and had taken her out for dinner especially to cheer her up. The restaurant had been top-notch and he'd urged her to have anything she liked. He'd had no appetite and sat smoking and drinking Perrier all night, going off when dessert arrived to 'make a call', then coming back to the table with that bright-eyed, tight-faced look that a line of coke will happily arrange. She was tired that night and didn't feel like indulging, but he'd been persuasive and they ended up finishing a gram between them by midnight. She couldn't sleep and they rolled around in the early hours, their white-hot energy gradually burning itself out until it was time for her to get up and go to work. Her head ached and her hands shook all day with that familiar hollow, nauseous chill and she vowed she'd never do it to herself on a weeknight again. Not that her job required a great deal of application, consisting of a lot of 'S*ure*, I think we can manage that's and 'That would be *great*'s, long lunches in cheap Italian cafés and a couple of drinks two nights out of five round the corner at a second-rate media haunt, the word 'haunt' being perfect for all the ambitious ghouls who drank there. Sean was some kind of thrill in her life. He completed a picture she'd imagined before she came to London of things that she believed made up a full life. The moments with him, however, were unreal, all stemming from a bag of synthetic dreams.

Now, as she sat sandwiched in between the others, a little stoned from the clouds of skunk billowing from the front, she idly mused on whether they could ever have a 'life' together; so far, it had merely been a nightlife.

They pulled up in the car park next to a white Golf full of preening swan-girls.

'W*here* is my bloody make-up bag?'

'Amanda, did Max sort out those farking Es or what?'

'Yeah, he's coming at twelve-ish. He got that "dealer-friend" of his to get us some capsules. Apparently, they're *really* farking strong.'

'*Excellent.*'

'OK, GUYS . . . I'm leaving the duvet here if anyone wants to catch some zeds later on.'

'I farking *knew* we should have booked a room.'

Lee expertly stared the girls out in disgust as they tottered up the drive, long golden legs burnished by recent Caribbean sun and glossy Michaeljohn hair. They glowed with the benefits of leisure overtime.

'I'd like to see the state of them come morning,' she bitched as they traipsed up behind the girls. '"Dealer friend" indeed . . .'

The huge house had been transformed into a modern pleasure palace. Huge, mutant Day-glo flowers covered the walls, framing the portraits of disapproving aristocrats who sneered at them as they climbed the stairs to their room.

'I don't like yours much,' giggled Kerry to Lisa as they passed a sickly wigged-out and powdered fop. 'Look, his eyes are fucking following us, the creepy bastard.'

The door to Room 11 was open and the place was crammed full with bags, fags and electric anticipation. Philippe hogged the bathroom, putting the final touches to his outfit, an astounding arrangement of gold and silver floating panels. He looked like a Roman astrologer.

Gervase was panicking that he'd left his shades behind: 'I can't walk around in the morning with my scary E-eyes.'

Lee looked the business in a full-length, pistachio Ben de Lisi and delicate strappy heels. Kerry and Lisa looked at her in admiration.

'Ahhh, your mum'd be really proud if she could see you,' cooed Lisa affectionately.

'Yeah, bless her . . . This one's for you, mum,' replied Lee, chucking a pill in her mouth.

They dumped their stuff and did a few retouches while Paul sorted out a bag of Es on the bed. Damien skinned up and Gervase cracked open a bottle of Moet. Around eleven, when they all felt suitably calm, they headed downstairs.

The main room glowed luminously. The decor was on a tropical theme, with fake palms, water tricks and grotesque life-sized monkeys swinging from the ceiling in grass skirts. The DJ box was a miniature Aztec temple and tequila-shot girls wandered about in gold slave outfits. Airy, hissing chords seeped through from the other room, where Key to Life's 'Forever' was blaring, a soaring, Hammond-organ-filled Garage tune. The place was perfect for a full-scale party, with passageways, hidden corners, windowseats and wide staircases to sit on.

Marly promised herself she would enjoy it whether Sean turned up or not. They danced in the main hall, the lights beaming down on a thousand or so happy sprites, all jumping for joy at their individual personal beauty. Marly longed to see an imperfect face, bar her own.

She and Paul went out for some air. They stood on

the stone balustrade and looked over the rolling grounds, lit by blue and green lamps. It was all flawless, yet she felt incomplete, as if everything before her was merely an illusion and real life was something far off in the distance. They sat and listened to the thump of the music coming from inside and smoked cigarettes and listened to the chit-chat of the group sitting on the grass below them.

'You going down Chislehurst Caves next week?'

'What's going on?'

'Del from Planet Plastic's doing a night there. Mel's got some guesties for it. Should be a blinder.'

'You got any of those pills left?'

'No . . . I just necked the last one.'

'Fuck . . . Well, give us some of that speed, then.'

'Nadia, are you still going to Ibiza?'

'Dunno . . . Charlie's finding out about flights. I hope so. Be nice to have the sun on my face again.'

'Yeah . . . and being off your face all night, ha, ha, ha . . .'

'I got my horoscope done by that bloke inside.'

'Yeah? What sign are you?'

'Double Gemini.'

'*Really*? What, your ascendant as well?'

'He said my love aspect's governed by Mercury, which means I'm really dominant in relationships, but my career's in Jupiter and that means I'm really indecisive . . .'

'Is that fixed or mutable?'

'Mutable, I think. It's all right, though – you know, for

my job – 'cause I've got to be really flexible for my clients and that.'

'Are you getting any money for that yet?'

'Well . . . no, not exactly, but, like, Kingsley, my boss, said he wants to take me away with him for a "business weekend" to discuss all that. He said he reckons I've got real potential . . .'

Paul raised his eyes at Marly and passed her his spliff. She took a long drag and let out a heavy sigh.

'What's the time?' she asked casually.

'Half-one . . . Is your, um, boyfriend coming tonight?'

'Boyfriend.' She laughed as she repeated the word out loud. 'I really don't know. He's got other things on, apparently.'

Paul said nothing, knowing better than to interfere in someone else's affairs of the heart. Instead he told her a story about a friend of his from home who'd once taken one too many Es and at the moment his fave tune came on in the club he'd had an almighty rush and 'over-gurned', dislocating his jaw. The worst part was explaining his problem when he got to Casualty: 'He's done what, sir?' asked the young doctor.

Unbeknown to Marly, Paul had an enduring fully blown crush on her. He'd kept his distance for the past few months for obvious reasons, but she'd been on his mind far more than he'd liked. He wondered if the attraction was simply due to her unavailability, but he'd certainly never felt like this before, and there was absolutely nothing he could do about it. From the first moment he'd first seen her in the downstairs hall of their flat and thought in that instant how fresh and clear she looked, to the gradual realization that she could be awkward and nervous but always gentle and deserved to be loved, she had pervaded his thoughts, always with a strong urge for him to pick the right moment for them, the feeling of saving her till last. He was not one to be instantly moved by a pretty face, but it was as if Marly's looks were an exact mirror image of her inner self. The memory of his first impression was untarnished, no matter how many of her moods or early morning hangovers he'd witnessed.

In spite of the strength of what he felt, he couldn't put a name to it. He'd been in love before, but that was not it. It was more an intense relief he felt whenever he saw she was at home and knew he would be in her company for the next hour or two. She listened like no one else and seemed to genuinely think about things she said and give honest replies. Before he met her he'd thought that relationships were easy to define: his family, his mates and, once or twice in his life, a partner. Someone you took on the responsibility of really knowing. She didn't fit into his tidy list. One night, on acid, he thought he had it all figured out that it was just a stupid desperation for something lacking in his life. He accepted that he'd probably never know how she felt and tried to forget his nervous heart and be happy for her.

Eleven

Wiz was getting turned on.

'Go on. Tell us what's so fucking great about it all, then?'

The babe shivered in her white ostrich-feather bra and Agent Provocateur cami knickers at BB's practised growl and her two male companions fell silent, looking in bewilderment at their captors, who stood in a menacing row in front of them, arms crossed, disguised in masks pilfered from their local toy shop's 'Zorro' range. Wiz had gone one further and bought a balaclava, although he was beginning to regret it in the stifling heat of the small back room of Baz's office.

'What do you mean?'

'What I mean, *darling*, is why do you feel the need to ponce about like a fucking parrot on heat, and more importantly, *how* can you listen to that heap of old shit and actually feel good on it?' Wiz stood back proudly. He'd been rehearsing his line and felt confident that he'd achieved a suitable degree of sabre-rattling in his tone.

'Hey, look, OK, whoever you are, just don't speak to her like that, all right?' one of the boys spoke up bravely.

'I think she's fucking well fit,' whispered Col to Baz.

BB leant down until his nose was almost touching the boy's face and smiled a slippery smile.

'It's for your own good, mate. We don't enjoy this, you know.'

'Well, why are you doing it, then?' said the second boy with a half-laugh.

'Because it's our duty to put a stop to mindless chants and boring fucking confining beats that dull your taste and make you think you're satisfied with that you're getting. It's low quality, like fucking McDonald's, and if someone doesn't put a stop to it soon, real music's going to die.'

The others looked with admiration at Virgil as he sat down, exhausted after his mini Nuremburg.

BB cued Wiz to start up the music and the proce-dure ensued. It was now as natural to them as their ABCs (at least, to some of them, Wiz always having a few problems after the letter P). In the past month they'd hit three clubs with tactics varying from subtle joke-shop-style tricks, including exploding spliffs passed on to unsuspecting happy clubbers on the dance floor, to the more serious hostage nights at Col's dad's lock-up or their present hideaway, Baz impressing his boss by asking for the keys so he could 'explore a few ideas he had for revolutionizing the car-valeting industry'.

Curiously, to the others at least, BB never wanted to actually take part in any of their missions *inside* the clubs, his explanation being that he should preserve his role as 'mastermind' in the van outside, giving the orders and thinking ahead as to their next move. 'Lazy fucking git, more like,' grumbled H. But the truth was BB didn't trust himself inside those places any more. The thought of a repeat of that fateful night was a risk he couldn't take.

The AHL's regular appropriation of handbag 'innocents' was making ripples all around town, even warranting a mention in the latest edition of H*it the Decks*, which Baz cut out and proudly framed on the wall. One club was now beginning to issue cautionary messages on its flyers, much to their delight.

Back in the room, the girl was beginning to suffer.

'Please, I really need the loo. Can't I just go quickly? I'll do anything you want.'

'Oh, yea?' Baz laughed a smutty laugh, which quickly turned to an embarrassed cough at a stern look from BB.

'Don't start trying it on us, love,' he warned her.

'For God's sake, let her go. She's not going to –' began the first boy.

'Shut it,' snarled Wiz. 'He keeps on asking for it, Chief.' He looked at BB.

'Why not let me work him over a bit – nothing rough, maybe just rip those horrible buttons off his Versace shirt.'

BB held up his hand in a calming gesture.

'All right,' he said to the girl. 'Somebody better go with her, though.'

'Me,' came the chorus.

BB sighed. 'I'll take her. Virg, I'm leaving you in charge.'

Virgil nodded sharply and pulled up a chair, sitting astride, staring at the boys intently. He signalled H to turn up the music. The caustic, biting sounds reverbed around the small room, with grating Les Dawson piano chords that caused the two hostages, with their untrained ears, to wince painfully. Wiz hid his disappointment, thinking he had always been BB's second-in-command.

The loo was in the basement near the fire exit. BB walked directly behind her as they made their way down. He wished the night was over, suddenly feeling exhausted, and made the mistake of yawning.

'You look like you need a little nap. Why don't you have a lie-down. Go on, I won't tell the others.' She smiled coyly.

'Come on. Just do what you've got to do,' he snapped.

'You know, I really don't understand why you're so against people like us. If you'd been in that club tonight with us, you'd know what a laugh it can be. It's just about feeling good, letting yourself go –'

'Shut up, will you.' He couldn't bear it. 'When was life ever about feeling good. It's you who doesn't understand. There's more to it than just having a good time, you know.'

The girl looked at him blankly. 'Like what?'

'Well, like having some musical integrity for a fuck- ing start.'

The words jarred in his head as he remembered how he'd secretly slipped in his shameful handbag tune on the DAT he'd sent to Holland along with the boys' techno track. He hadn't meant to, but in a moment of blind ambition thoughts of commercial via- bility had strayed into his mind.

'Just get in the loo and hurry up.'

Marly shivered a little on the cold stone floor of the big house.

'Shall we go and find the others? I could do with a drink.'

Paul, lost in his own thoughts about her, looked up with a start.

'Huh? Oh, yeah . . . Yeah, I wouldn't mind hearing Rogan Josh's set.'

They found the others sitting in a huge group by the fountain in the main room. Lee was teetering on top of the big fake rock in the middle of the pool.

'Look at her. The fucking Venus di Chingford,' Gervase cried, clapping his hands.

'Oi, it's Colchester actually, you ignorant bastard. Push him in, Lisa . . .'

Marly couldn't help herself. She went to see if there was any message at reception from Sean. The girl shook her head, and at that moment a big chattering troupe of people arrived through the main doors. Sean was arm in arm with two girls who looked like they'd been around the block a few times and then gone back to kerb crawl. Sean was oblivious to her and walked straight past to go on up the stairs. It was Dani, trailing behind the others, who spotted her.

'Honeeeey.' She sprang a big kiss on her, all rolling eyes and slurred drawl. Marly wished she could tell her they really weren't worth it. 'Thank God you lot are here. I mean, I know Oliver invited me and everything, but he's acting really wierd tonight.'

In other words, he doesn't give a shit, thought Marly, I know the feeling.

Sean suddenly turned back on the stairs and saw her. He came down and gave her a kiss that felt practised and artificial. Dani raised her eyes and made a big show about leaving them alone.

'Well, I made it. Having a good time?'

His face was set in a tight grin and his eyes darted everywhere but her.

'Yeah. Kate and the others are in the big room. Coming in?'

Sean was distracted. He looked up towards the stairs, where the others were waiting.

'Listen, I'm just going to nip up and change first. I've been in that bloody studio since eleven this morning. You go on. I'll see you in a bit.'

He patted her on the shoulder as if she were a child being sent to play and strolled off. Marly wandered into the vast, thundering hall, pushing her way through the whooping, heaving pit of dancers and wondered what to do.

'I'm over-reacting,' she told herself. She always freaked herself out on drugs and it annoyed her. Weren't they supposed to lift the weight *off* your shoulders.

Kate came over and put her arm around her neck.

'I can't help it. I know it's a shame-up but I do go all gooey when I've done a couple of doves. Are you all right, darling?'

'Yeah . . . These are nice pills.' Marly tried to get caught up in the music to take her mind off Sean.

'They certainly are,' replied Kate, linking Marly's arm. 'And in my professional opinion, I'd say we could do with a couple more.'

By half-five, people were heading outside to sit in the grounds and look for the magic mushrooms that were still in season or piling downstairs to the swimming pool and Jacuzzi in the hotel basement. The shallows of the pool were crowded with bodies in various stages of undress, wading in the shallows, too out of it to actually swim. The girls stripped to their underwear and jumped in the deep end. Paul, Damien and Lucy watched laughing. Marly and Lee swam up to the other end and sat on the side, accepting a joint off a stranger.

'Hi, I'm Guy,' he said good-naturedly.

'*Really*? I'm *so* pleased for you,' said Lee loudly.

'Oi, Gervase,' she called as he walked out of the changing rooms wearing a pre-swim kaftan. 'We got one of your sort down here.'

Marly smiled at the boy helplessly as Lee swam off with the joint in her mouth.

'Sorry . . . It's her birthday.'

Guy's friends were comparing body piercings on the side of the pool. One boy pulled down his trunks to show off his prized possession: a three-inch metal bolt inserted through the tip of his penis. The enraptured audience ooh-ed and aah-ed, craning their heads to get a better look.

'I've got mine done too,' piped up a serious, straight-looking woman of about thirty.

The crowd suddenly swelled in numbers. Marly got out of the water and borrowed Guy's towel. Guy took this as a signal that his luck was in. Lee clocked him and started pretending to French kiss Marly in front of him. He suddenly remembered he had to find someone upstairs.

They sat on the sun-loungers and sent Philippe off to the room to get some of their booze. He came back with three bottles of wine and a message that Sean was looking for Marly. He was in the upstairs bar, Gervase confided cosily.

The bar was steamy and smoke-filled. The floor shook with tremors of bass erupting from the huge black speakers. Marly spotted Sean at the far end, sitting between two wasted waifs. They all looked miserable. He raised his eyes slowly as she approached.

'Hello, stranger.' He got up unsteadily and gave her a big hug. 'I've been looking for you everywhere,' he said unconvincingly as he ruffled her hair.

'I've been swimming.'

She had a sudden urge to get serious, to ask: 'What are your intentions?' But her head was a racetrack of confusion, thoughts speeding round a hundred to the second. She couldn't risk sounding desperate.

'Do you want to go up to Oliver's room for a smoke?' He put his arm around her and kissed her clumsily on the mouth. 'You look gorgeous.'

Oliver was locking the door of his room as they approached, a pubescent model hanging off his shoulder and giggling impishly. 'We're just going in for a sit-down, mate. All right?'

Oliver tossed him the keys with a wink and a slippery smile, and stumbled off down the hall, dragging Velvet, as she introduced herself, behind him.

Inside, the room resembled backstage at the Palladium. Clothes were strewn everywhere, like deflated chorus girls in glittering rags. Sean pushed a heavy blond Astrakhan coat off the bed and lay down, pulling Marly with him. Her head spun and all she could feel were his hands moving over her back. His urgency startled her and as she closed her eyes the blackness under her lids filled with flashes and white stars. Unthinking, not even knowing if she wanted him, she followed his awkward movements. The muffled beat from downstairs seemed to seep into her, making them fluid and smooth. She felt power over her body, needing to indulge her wilful startled senses. He was more aggressive than she'd ever seen him. The pounding strains of the track playing downstairs filtered through the floor.

'Hmm . . . "Space and Time" . . . Heaven and Earth, top track,' mumbled Sean as he lay back against the pillow afterwards and curled up against her.

She wasn't sure if she liked this version of him. It made her feel she was with a stranger who neither knew nor cared for her. She wanted to shut out the encounter and wished sleep would cover her and replace everything with a dream. They lay in silence for some minutes. The music grew louder. Sean's hand kneaded hers in a rhythm, following the bass lines of the track.

Marly pulled her dress back on, smoothing out the creases, and Sean lit another joint and exhaled a deep sigh.

Say something, she urged him inwardly, willing him to start some kind of normal conversation, something that would make the whole thing more real. But he lay silent, blowing out clouds of sickly sweet smoke, and she realized it was just part and parcel of the night for him. Marly tried in vain to adopt the *Cosmo* approach, to disregard anything more than the mechanics, telling herself sex was no big deal. The build-up of these past months had given her fatal notions about the future for them. She began to understand now that in this wonderland, that was the one thing she wasn't allowed to hope for.

Sean went into the shower and said he'd see her downstairs.

She headed for Lee's room in a daze, hoping someone would be there to cheer her up. Paul, Damien and Lucy were watching a breakfast TV programme, drinking the remains of Gervase's champagne. They greeted her with smiles and Paul offered her a last slug of the bottle. Delia Smith's mumsy countenance appeared in close-up on the screen.

'You know, when autumn is upon us, I actually look forward to rainy days so I can lock myself away in the kitchen for a good old session of baking,' said Delia as she switched on her electric whisk.

Paul burst out laughing. 'Is *that* what they call it these days?' He was in a silly, trippy mood after half a micro-dot.

'I bet her old man's a right fat cunt. Imagine all them cakes she forces down him when she's trying out recipes . . . and, like, he'd never say no, would he? You couldn't . . . Not to Delia Smith's grub,' said Damien.

Lucy looked at them and smiled benignly, rubbing her stomach.

Two spivvy boys nobody seemed to know sat in the far corner of the room on a mattress, talking in hushed tones. Marly went to retouch her face in the mirror beside them. They assessed her slowly, then went back to their lines of speed.

'Mmmm . . . That's a *really* nice buzz,' said the first.

'Yeah, man, I told you the buzz was good on this stuff. Only a fiver, man, from George.'

'Yeah? R*eally* nice buzz. Better than that shit you got last time, man. You getting a buzz off it, man?

'Yeah, man. Top buzz . . . Oi, look –' He lowered his voice in the vain hope that Marly wouldn't hear, standing just a couple of feet away – 'Them birds are pretty fit, man . . . Look –' He gestured to Kerry and Lisa, crashed out on the bed, Kerry's skirt ruching up around her hips in her sleep. 'Look at them legs, man.'

'Yeah, man . . . Fit. I wouldn't mind having a bit of that.'

'What, like *now*, man? But, like, she's asleep, innit?'

'Yeah, man, I'd *really* like to have sex wiv her, man.'

There was a pause as they both looked at the girls with watery, longing eyes.

'Yeah . . . but that's like, rape, man.'

'What?' He paused in his stupor.

'Oh, yeah, man . . . S'pose you're right . . . This is a wicked buzz, man.'

Marly looked at them and laughed in disbelief. They

shifted uncomfortably, shaken suddenly out of their juvenile dreams. Shuffling their bits and pieces, they slipped their RayBans on in shame. Marly slumped back on the bed next to Paul and shut her eyes. It was strange how she felt more comfortable lying here than with the man she'd just been to bed with. Sleep escaped her, as the room was beginning to fill up now with assorted stragglers, all looking for a pillow or a patch of floor to lie down on and skin up.

Lee burst in with Oliver, who still seemed eager to make a conquest of her. Lee was playing hard to get. 'Always get them, love,' she whispered to Marly as Oliver chopped out five huge lines of coke.

Marly lay back and smiled as she listened to Oliver's self-absorbed rant.

'You know, among all this bullshit,' he droned nasally, 'I get *so* many girls, wherever I go . . . Goa, Ibiza, Frisco . . . who are just in it for the thrill. I mean, I don't wanna sound egotistical, but I know they just hang around because of *who* I *am*. It's kind of hard sometimes, you know, just sussing out who's for real. I mean, you're a beautiful girl and we have a laugh, no strings, and I don't feel like you're skanking me. It's nice to know that . . . For once I'm valued for my inner vibe, you know, as opposed to the public *me* . . .'

'Oh, yeah,' said Lee as earnestly as she could, schnozzling a huge line from his stash on the mirror.

The room was gradually filling up with various movers, shakers and gurners, all piling in looking for a refuge.

The curtains were still drawn, fooling the crowd into thinking the night hadn't ended. A well-known DJ came in and greeted Oliver, then sat on the floor with his girlfriend and together they discussed his recent set.

'No, something was missing. I *knew* I should have brought that Indo track. You know . . . R U Sleeping.'

'Babe, the set was perfect,' cooed the girl.

'It was the crowd . . . *they* were fucking dead. I don't know who put you on so late, but I'm gonna have a few words to say about it when I find out. You *know* you play best early on. I worked it out, OK. You were born at about two a.m., right? So that means you're a rising sign and that's the part that governs your creativity. Anyway, I'm gonna do your chart next time just to make absolutely sure . . . And I had this dream the other night, right? There was this half-moon . . . So just make sure you consult me on your next set.'

One of Gervase's camp club-character friends, best known for his appetite for outlandish outfits and young dewy-eyed males, had seized upon the two sex-criminal speedheads in the corner. 'You boys must come to our next party,' he said as he smoothed out his Astroturf ballgown. 'I'll get you guesties. We could do with a few more like you. Why don't you give me your number. I'll put you on the mailing disk.'

On the other bed were Scott, Melinda and Billie, impeccably dressed and coiffed, who seemed to know Oliver and were hanging around in the event of a free line. They set about name-dropping in loud voices, arguing over B-list celebrities and their love-lives as if they knew them intimately. At present they were crucifying the new presenter of a popular youth programme.

'I mean, who's he fucking trying to kid? Doing anti-drug shows when we all know he's a Charlie fiend.'

'Tell me about it . . . Up until last month he was *dealing*, for Christ's sake.'

'You remember that pop promo I styled last week? It was leaking with the stuff. I never knew what the title "line producer" really meant – know what I mean?'

The trio threw their heads back and roared.

Lee and Paul were making up names for the worst house compilation album in the world.

'Yeah, you mean *your* album, Paul,' Lee teased.

'What about . . . *Gonna Blow Your House Down*?'

'No . . . *Country House*, a house anthem collective with Kenny Rogers on vocals.'

'No, Billy Bragg samples and we call it *Council House*.'

Lee was feeling very up, while Oliver was trying to feel her up. She took full advantage of the situation by groping round his crotch, looking for the rest of his coke. Oliver seemed to find this highly amusing.

'You won't get round me *that* way, young lady,' he chuckled.

'Oh, yes, I will,' she said, glancing scornfully at the bulge in his trousers. 'It's only a little side-road.'

Everyone laughed as Oliver blushed and hurriedly excused himself to the loo. She chopped out the last line and asked Damien if he wanted half.

'Does the drummer of Def Leppard swim in circles?'
he said with a grin.

Lee passed him the mirror and put her cigarette out
in a nearby teacup.

'Has anyone noticed how good teabags are to put
your fags out in. I'm going to invent something, call it
the "Bag-Ashtray". We could do a deal with Tetley's
and have them cartoon blokes, Sidney and them, all
smoking fags and drinking tea first thing in the morning and using my "Bag-Ashtray" . . .'

'You always did have the brains in the family, Lee.'
Damien laughed, spluttering on his coke and sending
a fine white spray all over the bed.

Marly marvelled at older clubbers like Damien,
thirty-somethings still doing what they'd been doing
at fifteen: 'having it'. They'd been toughened up by
long-term boozing and drug habits and still managed
to keep up an eternal sparkle. The bright young things
around them had nothing on these die-hards. They'd
lived through punk and maybe even the original hip-
piedom and embraced all the new scenes that came
along. They'd experienced the time the new genera-
tion saw in retro films or magazines and tried to emu-
late the style. What they finally settled on was close,
but it was not the same. Nothing would ever shock the
world in quite that way again.

Marly told herself to be cool, but her heart was pounding heavily and she felt like throwing up. She got up
from the bed unsteadily.

'You all right, babe?' asked Lee, noticing how pale she'd suddenly gone.

'Yeah. I just need to, um –' She couldn't finish her sentence and stumbled out into the hall. She'd go and talk to Sean.

His door was still open and Marly peered into the dimly lit room. She heard his heavy, even breathing. He lay on the bed in a dead sleep. She looked at him for a long while, then closed the door with a sigh and decided to get some air.

'Anyone want to go for a walk?'

Back in Lee's room she sifted through the big pile of coats on the bed.

'I'll come,' Paul volunteered. 'I said I'd get some mushrooms for the boys.'

They climbed the hill next to the hotel. It was bright and beautiful, with the early sun streaming down, buttery gold, on the wet, dewy greenness. The sky looked like it had dropped acid, shooting hilarious coloured rays over the horizon. Marly breathed in deeply, a torrent of icy air assaulting her fragile nostrils, feeling the drowsy warmth inside her suddenly breaking up. She rubbed her eyes, which felt sunken and hollow, all traces of make-up long smudged away.

'God, I bet I look like shit.'

Paul, crouching down on the grass and poking hopefully at a tiny, creamy cap, looked up and grinned. 'Umm . . . Yep.'

She laughed and gave him a shove, sending him rolling down the steep hill into a heap at the bottom.

She ran down after him and knelt down. He wasn't moving.

'Oh, shit, Paul . . . Are you all right?'

He stirred slowly and groaned. 'No . . . You've squashed my fungi.'

The journey home was bleak. Marly, against her better judgement, had blown up at Sean in a disastrous 'confrontation scene'. Feeling teary and insecure, she'd turned on him and asked all those questions that shouldn't need to be asked if all's well between two people.

'What exactly is going on with us?' She'd cringed as soon as she said it. 'You turn up in the middle of the night, then grab me like that . . . For all I know you could be seeing someone else.' Then finally, 'I just don't know anything about you, Sean.'

He'd looked at her and smiled his easy smile. As usual, he was infuriatingly relaxed.

'There's nothing to know. This is it.'

Marly sighed. This wasn't what she wanted to hear.

He put both hands on her shoulders in a tired gesture. 'Look, I think you're ace. I just want to have a laugh. I thought you were up for that too. You're not looking for the romance of the century, are you?' he joked, unsuccessfully.

'No, of course not,' she said as confidently as she could, but privately she couldn't bear the thought of a future full of nights like this, drug-fuelled romps that didn't mean very much at all.

Sean was one of those rare creatures who made no emotional demands on anyone and expected none in return. Marly suspected he'd suffered over something in the past; perhaps it was tied up in the little boy in the photo. It seemed he lived in such a self-sufficient shell that he steered clear of anything deeper than the proverbial 'good time'.

'The thing is,' said Sean avoiding her eyes, 'I've got this sort of ex-girlfriend . . . She's really unstable at the moment. I've tried to break all ties with her . . . but it's really complicated . . . I feel like I should –'

Marly switched off at this point. She suddenly felt like smashing his face in. He left the next afternoon and said if she wanted to give him a ring he'd be happy to see her. It was one of those perfectly polite invitations you give to virtual strangers on holiday.

Marly cried that night, despite the 'prescription' of drugs Lee stuffed down her throat, and she felt she was going temporarily mad. She wondered if she'd asked too much of Sean? These past few months she'd felt like a different person every day. She wasn't even sure of the truth of her emotions any more. Recently her days seemed to swing like a pendulum between a mid-drug/post-drug state. Clarity of narcosis had a grim murkiness of its own.

She spent most of the journey home thinking about Sean and their strange times together. It burned into her brain and began to become a part of her memory, the way sensual things do, like the smell of a rose or the sea.

Twelve

AHL. TECHNO OR DIE

The poster looked good. Its bold red and black lettering, designed by Virgil on his computer, had just the right note of dread. Reminiscent of the old 'Smashing the NF' campaign was going to visually ram the message down the public's throat.

'What d'you think, Chief?' asked Wiz as he unrolled the first, crisp poster and pinned it proudly to BB's bedroom wall. 'I made up the slogan and Virg did the drawing.'

'Artwork . . . Its *artwork*,' Virgil corrected him testily.

'Yeah. Nice one. Very, er . . . menacing,' BB mumbled without looking up.

The boys had piled round unannounced to show him their various new campaign ideas and give reports on their recent successes or failures in their appointed tasks. It was, however, as much a social call as anything. Recently they'd been very concerned about BB's listlessness. It wasn't right, said Virgil sensibly, for a captain to flag in front of his troops, and the others had agreed.

'Maybe he just needs something new to happen. Maybe it's up to *us* now to get things moving,' suggested Wiz, secretly desperate to have more control of the group.

Silence fell in the room.

'Me and Col did some of them stink bombs down at the Satin Subway the other night,' offered Baz after a long while.

'Yeah,' giggled Col. 'That was ace. You should have seen all them fucking ponces choking and coughing and all the girls' make-up running down their faces. You would have loved it, Guv.'

'Yeah, I'm sure . . . Well done, boys,' said BB half-heartedly, as he sifted through old DATS in his desk drawer. He wished they'd go and leave him to get on with some music. After all, that was why they had come together in the first place: to challenge the corruption, the destruction of purity, in music.

BB had actually quite liked house in the early days – Derrick May, Adonis, Donny . . . those strong bass lines and catchy samples – but had turned off as the over-sentimental had filtered in, trying to get the dance floor excited over thoughless, repetitive tunes just because they were out of their heads.

Now, much to his surprise, he found he didn't really care as much as he once had. That recent exposure to popular 'club' music had taught him that to keep music pure you must keep it underground, that art and entertainment were not always the same thing. The music in those clubs that they once wanted to destroy was the equivalent of Australian soaps on TV, addictive and trashy but easy to digest.

He didn't *want* the world and his wife listening to his kind of techno, because it simply wouldn't be his any more. Music was BB's life, but he understood that work and play were two separate things. He'd make money from music one day, but it wouldn't necessarily be music he liked or respected. Somehow, in the last few months, BB felt he had finally grown up.

'What's the plan for the run-up to Xmas, then?' asked H, impatient to get back to Simone. She'd recently been giving him the slip, going off for regular nights out with 'the girls'. He was suffering from the 'turned tables' syndrome and wanted to know exactly what she was up to tonight.

'Umm . . . To be honest, boys, I haven't really had time,' began BB.

Wiz seized the opportunity. 'If I may –' He looked inquiringly at BB, who suppressed a smile as he nodded for Wiz to continue. 'I've been doing a little research and it seems there's a big Hit the Decks party on in the old film studios. All the big names are going. Looks like this could be the big one. Think about it, we're talking top handbag DJs. The very source of the evil – I mean, problem.'

The others gave their assent, while BB remained quiet.

'What's up, mate?' asked Virgil.

'Nothing . . . Look, are you all sure you want to do this? I mean, some of these DJs have minders and that. It could be tricky.'

Wiz began to get agitated.

'What do you mean? We can't pass this one up. It's what we've been working towards all these months. This is our chance to really make a difference. Don't you see? They'll have to listen to us if we've got their stupid DJs.' His voice quivered as it neared breaking point.

BB wanted to tell them all, then and there, that he'd had enough, that he didn't care any more about the cause. He wanted them to understand how pointless it was. A few months down the line there could be a new wave washing over London's clubs. Music came and went as fast as lightning. Why couldn't he come out and say it to them?

He'd come this far and to deny the beliefs he'd once felt so strongly would be a crime they'd never forgive. Just this one last job . . . then he'd break it to them gently. He made a silent vow to himself, took a deep breath and took control for the last time . . . for the boys.

*

'OK, darling. See you on the 19th. Love to Helen and the kids.'

Nicky put the phone down on yet another besotted cameraman, having swung him for her latest low-budget film at an unprecedented reduced rate.

Marly sat at her tiny desk, playing with the phone wire and thinking about painting her room a different colour. She'd need an advance from Nicky for all the stuff, plus she'd started worrying about what to get her family for Christmas, which was looming round the corner. Her head was pounding from the night before. Lee had dragged her along to Oliver's flat to watch his pop promo debut for an up-and-coming band. They'd ended up at the Underground and Marly wished she'd said no to that last E the lead guitarist had given her, but Lee reminded her musicians were normally so tight that she'd better take advantage. She needed a drink or a spliff to slow down her pulse.

The radio in the office was tuned in, as always, to Kiss. Marly guessed this was Nicky's attempt to persuade every visitor or client that she really was still quite young. The DJ told her in his hysterical gabble there were only twenty-odd shopping days left. By the harassed look on Nicky's face, as she scrabbled around frantically in a pile of papers, Marly guessed now wasn't the time to make her request.

Work was, on the whole, pretty unsatisfying. Marly read scripts that came in daily by the dozen and wrote depressing replies of rejection to writers, or filed away the hundreds of CVs from eager media graduates all looking for a way in.

'Darling,' Nicky crooned from the small, designer-chrome bathroom, 'you wouldn't nip round to Metro and pick up those rushes from the commercial. Eric's coming to collect them this afternoon and I just don't have time. Got to go and see my bloody director.'

Marly watched as Nicky slapped on her war paint, ready for another schmoozing session. She wondered what she was after this time.

'I need him to rethink those locations. Far too bloody expensive. They're all dreamers, darling. They think money's just a concept. Probably explains their bloody awful films. Right. I'll be back around five-thirty. Give Eric a cuppa if I'm late.'

She was gone, leaving a mushroom cloud of Eternity in her wake. Marly's stomach churned and she felt dizzy. She looked at her watch. It was nearly four. Metro didn't shut till five. Nicky's couch looked so inviting. She'd lie down for half an hour first, just a little nap . . .

She woke with a start to a loud banging. In her dream big cannons were going off and she was running across a field, followed by an army of angry Scotsmen. She was approaching a ledge and the only way was down . . .

Awake, she sat bolt upright and heard Nicky's voice through the locked door, screaming for Marly to let her in. The clock on the wall said half-six. The phone started ringing. She ran to the door and a red-faced Nicky stormed in, grabbing the phone, and glared at Marly. Eric was demanding to know what had happened to his rushes. Nicky's skills of tact and diplomacy came pouring out in a treacly-sweet torrent. She assured Eric she'd phone the guy from Metro at home and get him to open up for her. She put down the phone with an unruffled 'Ciao' and turned to Marly with a grim face.

'I'm so sorry, Nicky. I must have –'

'Save it. Look, I don't know what's wrong with you at the moment. You're in a dream all the time. I need you to *be there* for me, Marly. I need more from you. You *look terrible*. You've been late more times that I care to remember. If I'd known you'd be this half-hearted about the job, I'd never have let Nick –'

'I'll really try, I promise. Look, I'll meet the guy tonight and deliver the tapes to Eric myself.'

Nicky sighed and shook her head. 'Not the point, darling. I want you to decide if this is *really* for you, and if it is, I want you to buck up your ideas and make a big effort for me, OK, sweetie?'

Marly waited eighteen minutes for the tube that night and sat and scowled at everyone in her carriage. She could understand how easy it would be to just let yourself go in a place like London. Whatever your problems, real or imaginary, the city sometimes seemed full of scary monsters. Time, money, work, fashion, romance: pressures mounting steadily, like the piles of rubbish on every street, and they reared their ugly head at rush hour most of all. Thousands of Londoners, all struggling to keep their tempers, controlling unspeakable urges of violence and destruction. At least that's what Marly liked to imagine was lurking behind their meek exteriors on the long, boring Northern Line trek.

The sky threw down sheets of black rain as she ran from Chalk Farm station to the flat. A builder's van swerved to avoid her as she crossed the road blindly.

'You stupid fucking cow! Why don't you –'

The rest was lost amid the drone of traffic.

Days like these dragged her down. They made the idea of escape, by whatever means, irresistible. All she felt like doing now was getting in and getting out of it with Lee, Paul and Kate. The concept of 'home' in London was finally beginning to sink in. Every night she looked forward more and more to the flat and her life there. It gave her a sense of belonging in the big city that she'd always hoped to feel.

She still got a slight thrill out of spending evenings with Paul, with his funny patter about the TV, showbiz gossip, the news. He was always full of ideas of how to improve life.

'They should have fucking Russell Grant doing a spot on *Crimewatch*,' he said that evening as Marly finally sat down in front of the TV with a cup of tea and a spliff. 'He could sit there and give out the burglar's star sign and weekly reading . . . "Now we're looking for a luscious, law-breaking Leo. Now he tends to hog the limelight, a little prone to showing off, but, ooh, what a great lover and ever so generous."'

Paul also had a great fixation with kitsch, once coming home from the market on a Sunday, albeit after a Camden pub crawl, with a bag of tiny plastic nurses, kitted out in sexy *Carry On* uniforms and each bearing the mark of origin, 'Made in Taiwan', stamped in tiny letters on their bottoms. Paul couldn't get over his 'find' and set them out proudly in legions on the mantelpiece.

Marly liked his strange side. He was into everything and anything, a stimulus for a full life if you hung around with him. Nights out, days in, chatting to mates all over the place, he was eminently likeable and entertained for hours, expounding theories on the government, the universe and, above all, drugs and music.

Tonight he proceeded to show Marly his record purchases of the day. He took each one out proudly, enthusing wildly about break beats and bass lines, she hadn't a clue where each name came from and marvelled that he could remember so many obscure and apparently meaningless words.

Boys, she thought to herself, seemed to feel that need to gather information for information's sake. They were like spiders building up webs of fact and figures, learning off data by heart and all competing against one another to amass the biggest, most impressive collection. External knowledge was all, it seemed, and the one with the most was the winner.

The phone rang. For a trembling minute Marly simultaneously feared and hoped it might be Sean. It wasn't.

Kate had met a new bloke at Club Zero the previous Saturday, while being sick in the men's loos after too much Charlie. He'd cleaned her up, seen her home and taken her number. Since then they'd had two dates and Kate was on top of the world. Marly was pleased she'd found someone as nice as Keith, despite the name. Paul, however, reminded her there were *some* un-Keith-like Keiths in the world. Marly agreed charitably, even though she could only come up with Keith Richards. As Kate gushed and gabbled to her Keith, Marly couldn't help feeling a little depressed that things hadn't worked out with Sean. It would have been nice to get a call from him, just to say hello. She'd been through enough failed relationships in her life to know it didn't get any easier, the old familiar sick feeling and sleepless nights. It was such a drag waiting for that phase to pass, because it always did waiting around for her life to begin again.

Kate came off the phone in a flurry, mumbling she was going out, and disappeared into her bedroom to get ready.

'Where's Lee?' Marly asked as Paul put on a record and switched off the TV.

'Dunno. That dodgy Oliver rang for her. He said he's doing a club tonight at Cazbars. He kept calling me Phil, the wanker.'

'She's probably gone straight there. He must have got her at work. What are you doing tonight?'

'Not much. I fancy going out, though.'

'Yeah . . . Me too.'

'Shall, er, shall we go, then?'

'You're on . . . Phil.'

Paul waited in the cab as Marly locked up. He was scared to say it, but things were going well at the moment. He'd laid down three tracks that week with Ad and Dave in the studio and was *really* pleased with two of them. Martin, his girlfriend had said, was out of the country, but he seemed to like their previous stuff and promised them a meeting with a distributor when he got back. All he needed from them now, he said, was a small initial outlay for the pressing and printing and they'd be able to put out copies in the shops by Christmas. Best of all, though, was that Marly seemed to have got rid of the 'older man'. Paul's jealousy had been doubly bitter. There was something about older men that was impossible to compete with. No matter how much of an idiot the bloke might be, girls seemed to drool over that vastly overrated 'carrot' of experience they dangled in front of them.

As Marly ran towards the cab, her skirt riding up her legs and her mouth set in a determined pout, a shiver ran up Paul's back. He wanted her so much, but *because* it was her, he wanted it to be the best thing he'd ever had. He could wait, he thought to himself as she climbed in beside him, he could wait for ever for someone like her.

They stumbled in at half-four. Marly was drunk as a fish and tripped over the telephone wire, smacking her head on the door-frame. Paul guided her unsteadily to the couch and examined her forehead, where a gloriously purply black mound had risen as if by magic. They'd left Lee in Oliver's dubious hands at his club. After a couple of grams she was always a little hard to deal with and towards the end of the night she had started getting bitchy with Marly and Paul, accusing them of ignoring her.

Kate was still out with Keith and was probably staying at his. It would be their first time, she'd said to Marly nervously before she left.

Paul made some coffee and brought out a half-litre of duty-free whisky his mate had brought him from France. They lay on the couch, Paul's legs sprawled over hers, but still with a fraction of distance between them that allowed them to be comfortable. He played her the finished DAT he was planning to give to Martin when he got back. She said she loved it. He wanted to tell her he thought he loved her, but it was out of the question. Those times when two people are close and intimate hold such promise, but somehow pride always intervenes with its twins of rejection and humiliation. He came so close that night to leaning over and kissing her and Marly knew, but somehow she couldn't bring herself to make it easy for him. Instead each was glad when, finally, they went to bed alone and realized that the future might hold something for them both to look forward to.

Thirteen

'SING HALLELUJAHHHHH . . . SING HALLELU-
JAH –'

Dr Alban was getting excited in a rather uncharac-
teristic un-Swedish manner. Marly, however, knew you
had to play these occasions very coolly. She saun-
tered around the room as if, while perhaps not owning
it, she at least had shares.

Kate, Lee and herself had planned all week what
they'd wear for tonight, sad as it seemed. She did like
looking good once in a while, though, and tonight she
was certainly getting a few looks. Then it occurred to

her that this could well be due to the fact that she was one of the few unfamous people in the place. How bland-looking most celebrities were off camera, without that special glint in their eyes that only a 2K studio light can bestow.

She pushed past a couple of immobile models at the bar, both striking well-rehearsed poses, and loudly ordered two pints. The two beauties turned and stared as if somehow offended at her request. She deliberately took a huge, macho gulp, let out a loud sigh of pleasure, burped and grinned inanely. They turned away in disgust.

A serious-faced boy, part of a newly celebrated pop group, stood on her right, drinking double Jamesons and glaring at the crowd with an assortment of various contemptuous looks.

'I didn't realize it would be so hard at the top . . . Sometimes I'm lying in bed and it suddenly dawns on me how *famous* we actually are and I just think, where do I go from here? And, yeah – I'll admit it – I have thought about suicide.'

Kate was over in the corner, trying desperately *not* to mix business with pleasure, but her boss at the magazine was looming over her, making sure everything was going smoothly. The magazine was in financial trouble, Kate had told them, its only salvation being a couple of heavy-looking Greek guys, dripping in gold, whose hobby seemed to be investing in young publications – 'Porn,' Kate had mouthed – and cheap cable channels. She had been appointed to keep their drinks and their egos topped up all night. Poor Keith was twiddling his thumbs in the corner, being aurally raped by a rampant gay TV presenter. He smiled helplessly at Marly as she crossed the room and she gestured for him to join them if he wanted.

As she approached the table, Lee was talking furiously with the singer of an up-and-coming Brit pop band. Marly suddenly twigged that he and the Neanderthal drummer were making fun of her.

'So, like, you're into massage, then? 'cause, you see, I've got this problem with one of my larger muscles . . . and, er, I was, like, wondering if you'd, like, rub it better . . .'

They both sniggered as Lee failed to pick up on the innuendo.

'Well, it depends how much you've been using it,' answered Lee earnestly.

This sent the pair into schoolboy hysterics.

'Maybe if you stopped putting it up your friend's arse, it might feel better,' snapped Marly to the singer as she handed Lee her pint.

Their faces dropped and they struggled to think of a put-down. 'Do you like it rough?' slurred the drummer lechily as Marly dragged Lee off against her will.

'What are you doing? They're going to be really big, you know,' protested Lee, her eyes bright and starstruck. 'I was just about to frisk them for some Charlie.'

By one o'clock the small venue was packed and throbbing. Everyone seemed to be 'someone' here, apart from the magazine staff and their guests. The music was a mixture of sultry high-energy house and disco, giving all the babes in the room a chance to strut their stuff like it was the last night on earth. A premature Christmas spirit provided that extra sparkle. Lee had got her hands on some pills and she shared them out excitedly.

'Merry Xmas, one and all –' offering them round like sweets.

Kate and Keith, holding hands cosily, declined.

'Oh, I get it. Now you're hitched up with someone, you don't need them any more,' Lee said in disgust.

'No . . . I just don't fancy it tonight. I'm knackered and I want to be able to sleep when I get in,' replied Kate, a little hurt at Lee's tone.

'Right, then, more for you and me, Marl.' She knocked one back greedily and popped the other in Marly's mouth. 'Come on. Let's dig out some lonely Charlie-head and keep him company.'

They danced non-stop for the whole of Babe with Beard's set, lasting a full two hours. The glamorous trannie DJ came off to loud cheers and air kisses from all and sundry.

'Who's gonna chop 'em out?' he shrieked as he made his way to the bar.

Marly suddenly felt hot and bothered, her head reeling after three pills and endless lines in the cramped toilets. She decided there was absolutely nothing glamorous in bending over a grimy loo seat to get an incredibly short-lived buzz that just left you wanting more. It was a little depressing, she thought, that she would now always associate the crème de la crème of drugs with the heady scents of urine and Vim.

Outside, the crowd was at its most naughty. It was the kind of do that put you off being famous. Two hundred egos all striving to show how much they deserved to be in the A-list constellation – loud, confident voices braying and laughing at each other's wit and wisdom, not realizing that their community was so small and ureal that it had very little bearing on the big wide world. Still, it was fun to watch, like a class of seven-year-olds who'd got their grubby little hands on the medicine cabinet.

The Es were strong. 'They're only doves, Marl,' Lee had said vaguely a few hours before, but Marly had never felt this out of it and her jaw ached as she tried to control her facial muscles. A wave of paranoia washed over her. She didn't dare check her face in the mirror when she went to the loo and suddenly panicked that everyone was looking at her. Two girls giggled as she walked past. Marly instantly imagined them pitying her. 'Look at the state of that,' she was convinced they were saying as she tried to find a dark corner to sit down and let the ride run its course. She was desperate for something to smoke to bring her down. She spotted Keith standing on the terrace outside and remembered the eighth he'd bought from Rover earlier that evening.

'Keith . . . Look, call me rude . . . would you roll me a bloody spliff . . . please.'

It felt like the best smoke she'd had in years. Keith was brilliant, giving her the run of his gear, buying her drinks and indulging her babble with an understanding smile. Kate came out to join them.

'You picked a real gem here, Kate.' Marly put her arm around Keith and gave him a squeeze.

'He has his moments.' Kate gazed longingly at him. 'You seen Lee?'

'No, but I wouldn't mind going soon. I'm getting a terrible headache. There's something in these pills . . .'

Marly found Lee outside the toilets, kissing a very coked-up, very married actor. As she neared them, she spotted the glamorous wife, walking towards the pair with a face like thunder. Marly yanked Lee off him as quick as she could. Her dress straps were down, the hem riding up around her waist.

'Look at the state of you,' said Marly.

Lee was furious. 'What the fuck are you doing?' she screamed at Marly. Her face was contorted and swollen. Marly didn't like to imagine how much she'd actually done, but something in her eyes scared her. It simply didn't look like Lee any more but savage and disturbed.

'LEE, WE'RE GOING,' she shouted at her as if she was a child.

'You might be. I'm fucking staying here.' She pulled at her dress, trying vainly to smooth out all the creases in her satin Liza Bruce. The actor's wife was almost on them.

'Come on. You're coming with me . . . NOW . . . Unless you want a bloody black eye.'

The wife was a big girl and, according to *Hello* magazine, worked out every day.

Keith helped them get a cab and they rode home in stony silence. Once in the flat, Lee stumbled into her room and slammed the door loudly. Marly, still wired, switched on the TV. She wished Paul were here to cheer her up. She sat through a terrible seventies horror flick in which a cast of hammy thirty-five-year-old actors played sexy teenage vampires, then endless Japanese cartoons until she found herself staring at the vacant blue screen, watching the colour change to a deep sea-green then an unearthly turquoise before she dozed off. She'd noticed recently how she didn't dream these days. She'd always thought that dreams were the mind's way of sorting out the day's problems. She wondered if that was why she always felt so lost the day or two after a binge.

She woke to the sound of coughing. A horrible gurgling sound coming from the bathroom, followed by gasping and choking. She ran in. Lee was bent double over the loo with blood coming from her nose and dribbling from her mouth. There was more blood on the floor and down her T-shirt.

Marly froze at the scene.

'My God, Lee. I'm going to phone an ambulance.'

Lee shook her head and waved her away. 'Oliber,' she croaked as she spat a mouthful of blood into the bowl.

'Look, you've got to get to a doctor. P*lease* . . . Let me call the ambulance. For God's sake, look at you.'

'No . . . Call Oliber . . . In my book.'

Marly got her a towel and grabbed the book from Lee's bedside table. The phone rang for what seemed like an age, then finally a sleepy voice murmured, 'Yes.'

'Oliver. It's Marly . . . Lee's friend. Look –'

'Oh . . . yeah. Hi . . . She's not here, if that's why you're ringing . . . God, what time . . .? Ohhh, God. Its five-fucking-thirty.'

'No . . . Look, she's *here* with me. Listen, she's in a really bad way. Can you come over?'

'What's she done now. Look, tell her to take a couple of Temazepan and go to bed. I don't know, you girls –'

'She's fucking coughing up blood. It won't stop. Please . . . she won't let me ring the ambulance. She got me to call you. What about that doctor mate of yours, Chesney or –'

'All right, all right, I'll give him a ring. Look, just make sure she doesn't choke or go to sleep. What's the address again?'

Back in the bathroom, Lee was as white as a sheet and slumped against the radiator. Her eyes were sunken and shut. For one awful moment Marly thought the worst.

'LEE . . . LEE, come on. Try to stay awake.'

Lee groaned softly. Marly cleaned up the blood as best she could and wiped Lee's face. Then she covered her with a couple of thick towels to stop the shivering.

'You'll be fine. Just keep your head up and try to steady your breathing. That's it. Slowly.'

'Owww.' Lee winced suddenly.

Marly looked down and saw that she was clutching Lee's hand tightly, in her panic squeezing it as hard as she could.

'God, sorry. Listen, Oliver's coming over with his mate. Just try to relax.'

'I'm really fucking sorry, Marly. I'm so sorry to lose it like this, it's –' She started to shake with sobs and brought on another nosebleed.

'Ssshhh, it's all right. I'm glad I was here, that's all.'

'No –' Lee blubbed. 'You don't understand . . . I'm sorry for being such a . . . a lightweight.'

They both raised a brief laugh at the awfulness of it all. Marly felt ill. She'd always hated the sight of blood and she could feel the tremors from Lee's heartbeat throbbing through her T-shirt.

Chester arrived first. He'd seen it all before and calmly lifted her up and carried her to her bedroom.

'She's very dehydrated. Can you get a pint of water, and a straw, if you've got one.'

He took a small plastic bottle out of his jacket.

'What are they?' Marly asked.

'I'm going to give her 5mg of Valium. That'll bring her heart rate down and she might sleep.'

'I really think we should call an ambulance,' said Marly anxiously.

'Fine with me, darling. Just give me a chance to get out of here first.'

Lee shook her head frantically. 'Let him deal with it, Marl . . . please.'

Oliver arrived then, hovering at the door as if he might catch something. He wasn't very good in these kinds of situation, he explained airily as Marly made them some tea. Chester joined them, lighting a much-needed cigarette.

'She should sleep soon.'

They all jumped as they heard the key in the door.

'Kate?' shouted Marly. It was Paul. He looked pale and unhappy, but his expression changed rapidly to horror as he walked into the war-zone bathroom.

'What the fuck's going on?'

Fourteen

Wiz fiddled nervously with his 'lucky mascot', a lurid Korean keyring on which was a picture of a young beauty whose clothes fell off when you turned her upside-down. It didn't work so well these days, due to too much manhandling over the years. Wiz wiped it with his sleeve and squinted to see her left breast in the van's dim light.

'I tell you, mate,' he whispered excitedly to BB, 'this is it. I can feel it in my bones. Top DJs . . . and they're going to be ours.'

'Yeah,' replied BB in a flat, small voice, wishing he was somewhere else.

The back doors suddenly opened and Virgil, H and Baz, appeared, dragging two young men, partially punch-drunk and dazed from the seeing-to Wiz had ordered in the club car park. The street outside was busy with clubbers, but no one seemed to notice the commotion.

'DRIVE,' screamed Wiz to Col as he struggled with the others to bind and gag the pair. The van rocked violently as they screeched off down the Marylebone Road heading west. BB sat up front with Colin, his head hung, feeling very much apart from the rest.

'Turn up the music,' shouted Wiz, and Steve Stoll's 'Perverted Truths', with its speedy, caustic percussion, came blaring through the thin partition.

'This is what it's about,' sneered Wiz to the baffled boys. 'None of your fucking nancy-boy tunes. You wouldn't get your birds dancing to *this* one, would you? EH? WOULD YOU?' His enjoyment was obvious.

'Go on, Baz. Get their wallets. Let's see what Saul De Sade and Nino Spector really started out in life as.'

Baz fumbled around their back pockets, as the boys wriggled in fear of what he might do. He fished the wallets out and threw them to Wiz.

'Well, well, well. Boys, let me introduce you to plain old . . . Derek Jarvis and Neil Bottom.'

The boys let out hoots of laughter. The younger captive mumbled something angrily behind his gag. Virgil lifted it up for a moment.

'It's Bot*ton*, actually. It's an N not M,' he protested angrily.

Virgil stuffed the gag back in his mouth. 'Oh, well, what's a bottom between friends? Huh, huh, huh,' he added, causing more hysterics.

They drove on through the night. The two captives looked around slowly at the boys and began to shake their heads to one another knowingly and smile. Wiz was outraged. They were meant to be scared.

'What's so funny? Come on . . . Do you want to share the fucking joke? Virg, take the gag off him.' He gestured to Derek, the older of the two.

He took a sudden deep, gasping breath as his mouth was freed, then looked at each of them slowly. 'You're that bunch of losers, aren't you? The ones going round kidnapping people from clubs. What is it you call yourselves? The Nazi Handbag Front or something?'

Wiz's indignation forced him to feebly slap Derek round the face.

'Oh, OWWW,' he said sarcastically. 'Is that the best you can do?'

'You want to know what I'd like to do to you –' Wiz suddenly pulled out his Swiss Army knife and flicked it open. Neil flinched. Virgil, H and Baz froze.

'Yeah, I though that'd make you change your mind. You just keep your mouth shut till we get there.'

'What's going on back there? shouted BB in a worried voice.

'Who's that?' called Derek.

'Come on, show your face. Or are you too much of a fucking coward?' He craned his neck to peer through the gap, into the passenger seat.

BB turned round to look them both squarely in the face, then at Wiz. 'Look, mate, put that away. They're not going anywhere. You can do your thing when we get back. There's no need for all that,' he said wearily.

'What's all this "you" business. Don't you mean "we". What the hell's going on here? Are you putting me in charge or what?' Wiz's eyes lit up as he spoke.

'Whatever you say,' said BB with a sigh and turned away.

The van screeched to a halt outside Wiz's house. His mum was on holiday in Lanzarote with her new boy-friend and Wiz had decided to make use of the garage while they were gone. He'd been reading up on the lat-est terrorist tactics in his *Forces to be Reckoned With* twelve-part magazine and had blacked out the small windows with bin-bags. He'd even dug out some old Army sur-plus gear belonging to Ray, his mum's latest 'friend', in his excitement, just in case 'something went off'.

Wiz had always longed to join Her Majesty's forces, but had failed the medical due to a long list of ail-ments, asthma and chronic short-sightedness being the main offenders.

Virgil, Baz and Col dragged the two boys from the van, with BB following sheepishly behind, hoping to blend in somehow to a dank and musty corner.

'Right, then . . . Put them on the chairs and tie them . . . good and tight now.' Wiz sounded like a bad character actor in a B-western.

Virgil had prepared a lethal cocktail of tunes: Basic Channel, III Phase's nasty 'Der Klang Der Familie', 'Sex Crimes against Mongols' by Spod . . . all hypnotic, compelling stuff for the AHL, hopefully agonizing torture for Derek and Neil.

Wiz stood back and grinned, looking smug and approving at the scene before him. He was feeling the control . . . the new king of the techno frontier. He waited for the cries of submission . . . They didn't come.

He looked frantically to Virgil. 'Can't you put something a bit bleaker on?'

Virgil shrugged and went to his record box. Ten minutes later they were being subjected to 'Ghoul Child' by Retarded Spanking and 'Sinister Mother' by Frankie Fellatio, even 'Bruised Kidney' – Anon . . .

Still nothing.

A slow but steadily growing smile spread on the DJs' faces. Wiz stamped his foot and reached for his knife.

'No,' came a shout. BB rose slowly from his seat in the corner. They'd forgotten he was there.

Wiz turned and snarled like a cornered animal. The others stayed where they were.

'Well, come on,' he screamed as BB went to stand by the two chairs. 'What does our almighty chief suggest now, eh?'

'It's no good any more,' BB began quietly.

Fifteen

Marly dumpled all her bags on the kitchen table. Those useless Christmas items that only seem attractive in the rush at closing time a few days before the big day. She poured herself a whisky from the last bottle of Bell's from Kate's work. There were no mixers, so she drank it straight, slowly with the odd wince.

Her taxi to the airport wasn't due until five and she switched on the TV to while away the hour.

Kate and Lee had been gone almost a week, Kate to stay at Keith's for a few romantic days before going home, Lee because she'd needed to.

'Just think of all the fun I'll be missing this week, eh,' she'd joked wearily as she hugged Marly goodbye. But there was no longer any sparkle in her eyes and she looked wan and pale.

She heard a key in the door. Paul came in and seemed surprised and pleased to find her there. He'd thought she'd gone that morning.

'I need some clothes to take to my mum's,' he explained, as if he had to.

'Where have you been?'

They'd hardly set eyes on him since the night Lee was ill. He'd come and gone quickly and quietly every morning and evening, to sleep and eat. Marly and Kate had put it down to the demands of the studio.

'I got myself a new job, labouring out in Harrow. It's a killer start-time . . . I haven't been doing much else.' He smiled but his eyes were downcast.

'Oh, right . . . Well, how's things at the studio?' She thought he'd warm to this subject as he always did.

'Um, yeah . . . yeah, you know . . . Listen, have you seen that blue T-shirt. The one I lent Lee?'

'You know Lee . . . You won't get it back without a fight.'

Paul disappeared into the kitchen to make some tea and after a few minutes he came out. He sat at the table staring at his cup, a cigarette burning a long tube of ash in his hand. He looked up and, before she asked, he spoke.

'Martin stitched us up.' It was clear he was having trouble telling her. She'd never seen him like this. 'It turns out he never paid that studio bill. Not once. He owed them a couple of grand as well . . . Me and Ad got down there last Saturday – you know, the night Lee was ill . . . All our fucking gear had gone.'

'Yeah, but surely someone knew –'

'Oh, yeah. There were a couple of blokes in the other room and they seemed to know all about it. Their boss had come down and sussed what Martin was up to and sent a couple of mates round to tell him to pay up.'

'Well, did they find him?'

'Oh, yeah . . . And he must have gone straight round that night with a van and cut his losses.'

'He can't get away with it. I mean, you went to school together, you must know his family, don't you?'

'I'll claim some of it back, I'll have to say it was nicked from my mum's . . . I could find out. I just feel a bit fucking sick, to be honest. If I set eyes on him . . . Anyway –' He sighed deeply.

Marly reached over and put a hand on his shoulder. 'Why didn't you tell us before?'

He paused and finally looked up at her. 'I don't know. I was a bit embarrassed . . . I mean, it's a bit sad not being able to see something like that coming.'

'Look, people are ripped off every day.'

'Yeah, but still . . .'

Marly's taxi was late and he carried her bags down and waited on the doorstep with her.

'I, er, got you something . . . I didn't know if you'd still be here.' He took out a small ivory box and handed it to her with a shy little shrug. Inside was a thin string of blue-green crystals.

'Oh, they're gorgeous,' she beamed.

'Well . . . you know, match the colour of your eyes and that.' His cheeks tinged pink and he looked at the floor as the cab pulled up.

'Eh . . . You phone cab for Barley,' shouted the cab driver.

'Yeah . . . that's me.'

'Yeah . . . that's her.' They spoke together and laughed.

She reached up and kissed Paul quickly, just missing his lips. As she jumped in the cab, she could still feel the warmth of his skin. Paul watched her drive off, rubbing his cheek.

Since BB's disgraceful show of compassion to Neil and Derek, he'd been outlawed somewhat by certain members of the organization, namely Wiz and to a lesser extent, Virgil, although the latter's complaint was due more to the abrupt end to what he had classed as one of his best sets ever.

As BB packed, he remembered with sadness that night when his soul had finally been unburdened.

'WELL, COME ON. WHAT'S GOING ON? YOU LOST YOUR BOTTLE?'

BB, wished Wiz would stop shouting. The room seemed to amplify his grating whine.

'I think we'd all like to know exactly what's happened to you, BB. And don't think we haven't noticed your recent lapse of interest in our operations.'

'Noticed what?' whispered Baz to Col, spellbound at the prospect of a bit of a ruck.

Neil and Derek, the by now vastly amused hostages, sat and watched the exchange like a tennis match.

'I just don't see the point in it any more,' BB had mumbled.

'WHAT WAS THAT? I think you'd better repeat that. I mean, I know I didn't quite believe my ears . . .'

Sarcasm didn't suit Wiz at all. Neil and Derek sniggered.

'I said I DON'T SEE THE FUCKING POINT IN IT ANY MORE. I mean, who's to say what's good and what's shit anyway?'

'He's right, you know,' said Derek with smug enjoyment.

'YOU SHUT UP,' screamed Wiz. 'And pray tell us, what's brought on this little change of heart? I mean, let's not forget how *passionate* you used to be about this whole thing. Your baby, you said, your whole life –' Wiz was stricken like a spurned lover.

BB sat down on a box of records with a heavy sigh. 'The thing is . . . I can't go on with this any more. I just don't feel the way I used to.'

'Oh, yea? Do go on. I know I can't wait for this –' Wiz lit a Marlboro and chewed on his fingernail violently.

'Let's just say I've become a bit Swiss when it comes to the whole music war thing.'

'Eh?' said Baz and Col together.

'Neutral. I'm neutral. I don't care what they listen to or play. It's got its place.'

The rest of the boys digested this piece of news in silence, staring at BB in disbelief.

'But . . . you can't be . . . *neutral.*' Virgil was baffled.

'Yeah . . . I mean, what about our tracks? I though they meant everything to you, Chief.' Things were slowly beginning to register with H.

'They did . . .' He paused and then changed tone. 'I wanted to tell you all before, but I just didn't know how . . . The thing is, I got a call from that bloke Rudi in Amsterdam –'

'Oh, nice one. Did he like the tracks?' Virgil was ecstatic.

'Well, yeah, he did. One in particular . . . but it was something I did on my own.'

'Oh, yeah . . . ? That turbo-boost sample and the 909 perc –'

'Um, no . . . not that one.'

'Well, what's it like, then? Go on . . . you must have a copy on DAT.'

BB felt in his pocket, knowing what lurked inside. Virgil had his machine here. He supposed this was as good a way as any to explain. He handed the tape to Virgil.

'I can't wait for this,' said Derek bitchily.

The intro could have been from either camp and Wiz and the boys listened blankly. Then out of nowhere came the vocals sample rattling around the room like a whirlwind, causing H to choke on his cigarette and Col's mouth to drop open wide. The track flowed on, strings, pianos, all upbeat and fresh like a summer breeze had suddenly flooded into the gloomy garage. Derek and Neil nodded their heads and tapped their feet as much as they could in their ligatures. Wiz stood slumped against the door, shaking his head and looking somewhat embarrassed for BB.

'I think you've heard enough.' BB slotted the tape out of the machine and slipped it back in his pocket.

No one spoke. Then Derek began, 'Nice one, mate . . . I think that's all ri –' but he faltered as the tension rose.

'The thing is, Rudi wants me to go over to work with him for a few months. I . . . I don't know what –' BB was lost for words.

Wiz lifted his head slowly, a mixture of rage and jealousy coursing through him. His heart was hammering like a jungle track. BB saw the flash of the knife as Wiz lunged towards him. He dodged and Wiz plunged the knife into his old space hopper, disfiguring the smily face and letting off a long, slow hiss.

Virgin and H held him as he struggled.

'You sell-out. First sign of money and you –'

'You don't understand,' said BB, trying to salvage something of their broken trust, but at the same time feeling like he needed to run.

'I was there.'

'You were where?'

'I was at one of their clubs . . . A fully fledged, full-on

happy house club. I just couldn't help it. I went in and I stayed all night . . . and what's more I enjoyed it.' BB took a breath after the strain of coming clean.

'So you're going?' said Wiz in a small, broken voice.

'Yeah, I'm going.' BB felt inexplicably emotional. The moment seemed to go on and on.

'Erm . . . Does that mean we can go too now?' piped up Derek, looking relieved.

The AHL looked at the pair, wondering what the next move could possibly be.

BB smiled at them all.

'Now there's no reason why we can't have one last fling.' He smirked as he moved towards the decks. 'Virg . . . Do your worst.'

Sixteen

The tube was crammed with the kinds of people you never knew existed and afterwards would never see again. Strangers got on and bored holes through other silent strangers for no apparent reason, the wordless vicious interchanges forgotten as soon as they stepped off the train. Fear and loathing lived in these carriages, transforming pleasant souls into surly misers. The man opposite Marly got up from his seat, leaving a copy of the *Sun* lying there. Three pairs of eagle eyes were upon it, the fat man, the tourist and the uniformed security guard. The thought of all three reaching for the paper at the same time was too embarrassing to contemplate in this small, exposed world, so it lay there untouched until a bag lady got on and delicately picked it up as she knocked her way through people's legs to get to the connecting carriage doors and was gone.

Two seats down a man was talking Peugot 205s with his girlfriend, a sombre, pristine woman with a bizarre Charlies Angels hairdo. He went on excitedly to the topic of interest rates and salary increases. 'But we'll be £2,000 a year better off, darling.'

Four scruffy teenagers scrambled on, all chewing mouths and rolling eyes. Marly guessed they were on solvents. Their vacant eyes stared at everyone and saw nothing of interest and began to muck around, tormenting one another for fun. The youngest, a string bean of about thirteen, was flicking the nose of the girl next to his.

'Look, leave it out, you wanker.' She had a kind of English gangly grace, an arrogant mouth, snub nose and masses of wiry dark hair framing a freckled face. He continued to clown around, winking at Marly and the other females nearby, and finally made her laugh, showing her criss-cross brace. Their friends, no more than fourteen, laughed at him too and kissed each other, all tongues.

It was seven o-clock. At home all her family would be at church now, for the Feast of the Epiphany, 6 January. Nicky had asked her to come back on the 3rd to start pre-production on a new film. She hadn't minded. There was next to nothing going on at home and she'd begun to feel claustrophobic with so many people coming and going. Lee had phoned her on Boxing Day and sounded calm and relaxed, though definitely more subdued than she'd ever known her. Paul had sent a card with a vague mention of coming back around the 5th.

As she let herself into the flat, she heard voices. Lee was sitting on the floor of the living room in front of the gas fire, staring into the blue-orange flames. Marly wondered what she was thinking. After the flurry of hugs and kisses, she told Marly about her holiday and how she'd spent the first New Year's Eve in seven years at home with her mum and dad.

'No, I wanted to,' she said, noticing Marly's surprise. 'We baby-sat Damien's new baby. She's lovely.'

Marly told her how she'd met up with her college mates in Dublin for the big night.

'Did you do anything?' asked Lee.

'What? Oh, you mean . . . No, not really. I drank a lot and someone gave me a line about six to keep me awake. I wasn't really in the mood.'

'Yeah . . . I know what you mean.'

'You know, it's weird. All these people I knew at home. All pretty straight, into drinking really . . . and now they're doing Charlies and pills like –' She faltered but from her face Lee looked like she knew what Marly meant.

'We've had about twelve calls since I got in. Philippe

and Gervase, Dani, Oliver . . . I told him I was washing my hair – I always wanted to say that . . . Paul called twice. He reckons he's coming back tonight. Sounded very anxious to know when you'd be back.' Lee smiled a knowing smile.

'Anyone else?' asked Marly, trying to change the subject and hide her pleasure.

'Oh, yeah. Sean. I said you'd call him back. Are you going to?'

'I don't know. Maybe,' said Marly, but she knew she wouldn't.

They made dinner and played music. The phone kept ringing. Philippe knew of a party, Dani was excited about a one-off night at Club Creation –

'I've got guest list,' she told them excitedly.

Lee's and Marly's reply became a standard 'Not sure what we're doing. We'll call you back.'

They sat with the burble of television in the background and smoked a few spliffs of grass Lee had left behind before Christmas and discussed the possibility of Kate and Keith getting hitched.

'I've got to get out of that job,' said Lee after a pause.

'I thought you liked that kind of set-up. I tell you, it's no fun tubing it up and back to town every day.'

Marly was surprised at Lee's seriousness.

'Yeah, but you enjoy it, don't you? I mean, the whole thing of doing a job well and that –'

'Yeah . . . there is that.' Marly cringed and made a brief promise to 'apply' herself more in the office.

*

Paul strolled in at ten and handed out some beers to celebrate their return. Marly watched him with a smile as he talked about his fruitful holidays, of the music he was planning to do in the coming month. He was all hope and enthusiasm and she suddenly knew she couldn't go wrong with him around.

Lee suddenly let out a shrill scream. 'Look, it's snowing.'

They ran to the window and looked out. Big, strange-looking flakes were tumbling thick and fast from the skies. Lee sighed with pleasure.

'Hang on a minute,' said Paul with a frown.

He opened the window wide, leant right out and looked up. He began to laugh and called to the girls to come and see. Two floors up, standing on the edge of the roof was Rover. His dreadlocks silhouetted against the bright winter sky, he stood laughing aloud to no one in particular and shaking a big box of soapflakes, which drifted out on the cold air and floated gently on to the street below.

'He's finally lost it, the weird bastard,' said Paul, delighted at the scene.

'Rover's Alternative fucking Christmas. Tripping off his nut,' Lee gave out a shriek of a laugh. Marly was glad to hear it back in its rasping glory.

'Christmas is over, Rover,' Paul shouted up to him.

'Not yet. Not 'til midnight.' He threw out another wave of white flakes, twirling fast and frantic over the roof's dark ledge.

'You been at those micro-dots again, Rove?' Paul's eyes narrowed with concern.

Rover stopped dancing and stood on the edge teetering unsteadily. He cast his eyes down at the three of them, flashing a wide smile.

'No, mate. Not at all. Stayed with my dad for the duration. He might be an old bastard, but he's a wise one . . . Sorted me right out. Listen . . .'

They bit the still air at his bidding.

'It's all here, all we need,' proclaimed Rover, looking from side to side as if to gaze upon these imagined delights. 'Bright souls, music, the stars . . .' he stared out into the blackening night.

Marly looked round and smiled at Paul and Lee's wide eyes and open mouths. She raised up her eyes, past Rover, towards the sky. These strangers had come to mean something to her. The word stranger was strange in itself. It seemed to suggest other people were stranger than she was. For years she'd tried to imagine something beyond the realms of the earth – the possible and impossible, God or the Aliens. Now, tonight, all over town strangers would be slinking around bars, clubs and streets, passing by thousands more strangers, knowing nothing of each other. They were all aliens in some way. Marly knew that whatever lay behind Rover's sky, Earth-friendly or not, it didn't matter. She was surrounded. Every man and woman is a star.

Havin' it through the years . . .

Syd Barrett

George Best

Biz Mark E

Leigh Bowery

George Clinton

Ian Curtis

Peter Cook

Captain Riz

Demented Are Go

James Dean

Divine

Marianne Faithfull

George III

Jimi Hendrix

David Icke

Chuck 'Orbit' Jaeger

Chaka Khan

'The King'

LL Cool J

John Lydon

John Lennon

Spike Milligan

Morrisey

Keith Moon

Sir Mixalot

Steve Marriot

Edgar Allen Poe

Reg Presley

Keith Richards

Ollie Reed

Viv 'Have a good time, all the time' Savage

Sigue Sigue Sputnik

Sly Stone

Tootie

Raymond Wallbank

Zorro

About the Author

Geraldine Geraghty is twenty-five years old and lives in London, writing and working on scripts and films. She refused to give us any more information than that.

"I first met Geraldine at a party in St John's Wood. She was sitting at this table with this rasta who was apparently one of the Tottenham Three . . . Another time I went on holiday with her to Marbella. Caned the whole time. Can I say that? We had to drink warm beer all week because the fridge broke down. It was a good holiday. We just hung out at this exclusive port, laughing at people with too much money and no dress sense." JW

"I was in this English Lit. seminar. Geraldine, who I didn't know, wasn't saying a word. Then this girl at the back started harping on about Ireland and the Irish. And Geraldine just let rip and took her to pieces. Another time we were living in this flat on the Finchley Road. Typical Geraldine. Rather than advertise that we had an empty room to fill she just went outside and picked up two Australians from the street. One said his Dad had designed the Sydney Opera House, so we were very impressed. They took us to the cleaners, of course. They crept out in the early hours one night and we never saw them again. They owed us hundreds of pounds in rent. We still get flashbacks about it every now and then." CD